LB

F
JAC

PICKUP LINES

PICKUP LINES

HOLLY JACOBS

THORNDIKE PRESS
A part of Gale, Cengage Learning

GALE
CENGAGE Learning™

Detroit • New York • San Francisco • New Haven, Conn • Waterville, Maine • London

GALE
CENGAGE Learning™

LIBRARY OF CONGRESS CATALOGING-IN-PUBLICATION DATA

Jacobs, Holly, 1963–
    Pickup lines / by Holly Jacobs.
        p. cm. — (Thorndike Press large print gentle romance)
    ISBN-13: 978-1-4104-3396-1
    ISBN-10: 1-4104-3396-X
    1. Large type books. I. Title.
PS3610.A35643P53 2011
813'.6—dc22   2010043195

Published in 2011 by arrangement with Thomas Bouregy & Co. Inc.

Printed in the United States of America
1 2 3 4 5 6 7 15 14 13 12 11

For Erin Cartwright-Niumata:
I'm so glad we had a chance
to work together.

And a special thanks to the
Smokey Mountain Romance Writers
for introducing us!

Finally, for Craig Warvel at Star 104:
It was a long time coming,
but finally here it is!

PROLOGUE

"This is WLVH, Lovehandles, where love is more than just a song. Today we're proud to announce another male contestant for our Pickup Lines contest: Ethan Westbrook. Ethan, you have one hour to call the station to qualify as a finalist."

Puzzled, Ethan Westbrook looked up from the computer and glanced at the radio. Had that disc jockey just said his name? He shook his head. He hadn't entered any contest. Either he'd heard wrong or there was some other Ethan Westbrook in Erie.

Small world.

He went back to punching information into the computer until the phone rang. He grabbed the receiver. "Westbrook Pharmacy."

"Ethan. Did you hear? Did you call?" his friend Barney shouted into his ear.

"Call who and hear what?"

"Your name on Lovehandles. You're in the

hat for the male contestant if you call in the next hour. So call."

"What contest? I heard my name on the radio, but I didn't hear why."

Barney was a good friend and a co-worker, but succinct wasn't a word that anyone who knew him would use to describe him. "Al's Auto and Lovehandles radio station are sponsoring a contest. Two people, a man and a woman; a battle of the sexes sort of thing. Don't you pay attention to anything?"

"What do they have to do?"

"They have to live in a truck — I think they said it was a Chevy, if that matters. Whoever holds out the longest wins it."

Ethan laughed. "I don't need a truck. My BMW is just fine, thank you."

He wasn't rich, but he was financially comfortable — comfortable enough not to need to live in a truck for an extended period of time. It sounded like the sort of contest that would appeal to the very young or the very desperate.

Ethan Westbrook was neither.

"Thanks for letting me know though."

"You're not going to do it? You're not even going to try for the final?" Barney sounded incredulous.

"No I'm not, but thanks for the call." Ethan hung up before Barney could continue to try to talk him into living in a truck. Some of the stupidest moments in Ethan's life had happened because he'd listened to Barney. But living in a truck? No, not even Barney could talk him into that.

He chuckled and went back to the computer, sure that Barney's call was the end of it. He didn't need a truck and he certainly wasn't going to make a spectacle of himself like that.

Oh, he'd had more than a few spectacle-type experiences in his youth, but he'd grown up. Well, mostly at least.

Ethan pushed all thoughts of his misbegotten youth and insane contests to the back of his mind and began entering the data again. He'd come into work early today to catch up, not to worry about some juvenile contest.

"Did you call?" Charles Ethan Westbrook Junior barked as he entered the small office cubicle.

Ethan glanced at his imposing father. "Call who?"

His father rolled his eyes. "Call the radio station."

"Oh, you heard." Ethan's derisive laugh came out as a snort. "Of course I didn't call. I don't need a truck, don't even want one if it requires that I live in it first. Why would any sane person want to live in a truck?" Before his father could reply, Ethan added, "The answer is they wouldn't."

Charles was every bit the professional — his salt and pepper hair brushed just so, his business attire perfectly creased, and the disapproving frown on his face speaking volumes — as he leaned over the cluttered desk. "I can give you a number of reasons. Topping my list would be publicity."

"Publicity?"

"The radio station is working in conjunction with the car dealership. They're covering the event from day one until the end. Can you imagine how many times you could mention the pharmacy on the air? And what if the television stations get involved? Do you know how much airtime costs? The pharmacy can't buy that kind of publicity. We couldn't buy it, but maybe . . ."

Ethan could see where this was going. "No way, Dad."

"This contest would be good for the stores. Westbrook is a small local chain and we need all the good PR we can get. When I handed the reins over to you, I did so because I trusted you to put the stores first. This contest is a way to get the Westbrook name in the spotlight; a spotlight that would be good for business."

Westbrook's four small stores had a hard time competing against the national chains. Charles was right — they couldn't afford to buy this kind of publicity. Ethan was responsible for the business now and he couldn't afford to let this chance go.

"Make the call," Charles said, any paternal pride once again neatly tucked away. "They're picking twenty male names, twenty female, and then on Friday they're narrowing the field down to two — one male, one female. You might not even win the spot."

Ethan faced the inevitable. There was no way he could let this opportunity pass without trying. The entire family earned their living through the stores and they all looked to Ethan to keep things running, to keep the small family chain floating in a sea of huge conglomerates.

Ethan picked up the phone and punched the numbers with a terrible sense of foreboding.

Could he be lucky enough to lose?

"Lovehandles, the station where love is more than just a song. This is Peter 'Punch' O'Brien and Judy Bently. Punch and Judy in the morning."

The husky female voice that practically screamed sensuality accompanied Mary

11

Rosenthal as she maneuvered her ancient Pinto through the rain-slicked traffic.

The storm didn't make a dent in her mood. Nothing could.

The last day of school had finally arrived and her spirits weren't just high, they were soaring. Oh, it wasn't that she didn't like teaching — she loved it. It was just that Mary had plans for the summer months — big plans.

She'd spent the last four summers taking classes and had finally earned her permanent teacher's certification. This year she wasn't doing a thing except reading, and she wasn't reading text books — not a one. She planned to read all the fun books she'd been hoarding, just waiting for the time and opportunity. Read and sleep. And maybe watch an occasional old movie on television. She added the thought of curling up on her couch watching Cary Grant to her self-indulgent fantasies.

Sometimes it seemed she'd spent her twenties in the classroom, either as a student or teaching her kindergartners. But not this summer. For three glorious months she was going to be totally selfish. She wasn't going to think about school, or even set foot in one.

Books, the beach, Cary Grant, staying up

late, getting up at noon — those were her plans.

Not even Gilda was going to get in her way. Mary was used to worrying about her mother — Gilda had a way of messing up her plans — but not this summer. Neither the rain nor thoughts of her mother could dampen Mary's spirit.

Gilda was dating a new man and should be distracted enough to leave her alone. Maybe this relationship would last the entire summer. The enticing thought warmed Mary's heart.

Just then the steering wheel jerked to the side, pulling Mary from her reverie. She gave it a little tug back on course.

Okay, there might be one tiny, little flaw in her happiness. This ancient Pinto was held together with sheer willpower and a whole lot of prayer. But she wasn't going to let her old jalopy ruin her perfect mood either.

It might be old, but it worked most of the time. And that's all that mattered after all, she reminded herself.

Oh, she could get a job in a public school and with the better salary afford a better car, but Garnerwood Academy was more than just a job to her, it was a community and the students there held her heart.

Mary might be looking forward to her summer vacation, but she knew by August she'd be ready to start a new school year.

The Pinto seemed to be behaving again and Mary grinned as she listened to a sappy love song on the radio. She hummed along, contemplating all the marvelous possibilities the summer held for her.

The music on the station ended and Punch came on. *"Well, it's Thursday and we have just two more contestants to draw for our Pickup Lines contest. Our two finalists will have a chance to win a brand new Chevy full-sized pickup, courtesy of Al's Autos and Love-handles. This hour we're pulling from the girls' basket."*

"Hey, who are you calling girls?" Judy blustered over the air waves.

"Hey babe, if the garter fits —" Punch started.

" 'Hey babe' me again, Punch O'Brien, and you're going to be doing the rest of this broadcast in a standing position. Just draw a name from the women's basket."

There was a crinkling of paper, or maybe it was the crackling coming from her engine that caught Mary's attention.

Crackling? That wasn't a normal sound, even for her Pinto.

A huge puff of smoke billowed from under

the rust-spotted hood and Mary's high spirits took a nose-dive.

"Here we go. The last female," Punch placed a heavy emphasis on female, *"contestant is . . ."*

Panic flooded Mary's system, but she managed to pull the car to the side of the road. The billow of smoke had become a curtain, blocking the rest of the traffic from view.

It appeared her car had finally given up the fight and was cremating itself.

"Great, just great," she muttered.

What was she going to do without a car?

Mary unbuckled her seatbelt and grabbed her bags, ready to flee the inferno.

"Mary Rosenthal."

Her head jerked toward the radio, apparently the only part of her car that was still working. Had they just said her name?

Judy's voice continued. *"Mary Rosenthal, you have an hour to call WLVH, Lovehandles. If you do, you'll qualify as a finalist in our Pickup Lines contest."*

The smoke thickened. Mary groaned and stepped outside to safety.

She was going to be late for school. It was a silly thought to have as her car died a painful death, but Mary prided herself on her punctuality. It would be hard to be punctual without a car.

She needed a car or, maybe better yet . . . a truck.

The radio was still playing as the smoke grew thicker. *"And then, stay tuned tomorrow for the big drawing where we'll all find out who our two contestants will be. Remember, they'll live in our Chevy pickup for as long as it takes. Who has the stamina to win — the man, or the woman?"*

A police officer materialized through the gray fog. "Ma'am, you need to move away from the car."

Mary followed the officer who pushed his bicycle a couple car lengths away from her smoking Pinto.

"Are you okay?" he asked gently. "Can I get you something?"

"Do you have a cell phone I can use?" she asked.

Her mother always said the universe worked in mysterious ways — and this time it appeared the universe was working for WLVH.

DAY ONE

Second thoughts?

Mary wasn't having any of them. No she was having *hundredth thoughts,* maybe even *thousandth thoughts.* Since the moment she entered Big Al's Auto showroom, doubts had been scampering helter-skelter in her mind.

There was a basic truth about herself that Mary understood with utter certainty — after all, she'd worked hard enough to make it the truth — she was a regular, everyday woman. She was quiet, almost shy. She was a private woman who never wanted to be in the spotlight.

She was normal.

Living in a truck wasn't a very normal thing to do.

The fact that she was at Big Al's ready to do just that made her nervous and tied her stomach in knots.

She looked at the huge maroon truck and

fantasized about climbing into the pickup through one door and then climbing right out the other. She could ride the bus, or she could take a taxi. There were options she hadn't even begun to explore.

She should go.

Or she could do this one very abnormal thing and take a chance for once.

"So, Mary," the disk jockey said, "are you excited?"

He thrust the microphone in her face, waiting for her response.

"No, terrified," she admitted.

Terrified of making a fool of herself. Terrified that this one tiny step would be the step that led to her downfall.

An image of her mother — her very eccentric mother — flitted through her mind, but thankfully Punch's angelic smile distracted her. With a face as beautiful as his, he should be on television, because hiding that face in a radio studio was tantamount to a sin.

"Do you think you're going to win?" he asked.

"It's not a question of *am I going to win?* You see, I *have* to win."

She had to do this, she reminded herself sternly. Her Pinto was dead. It had been a glorious death. First the thick blanket of smoke and then, right after she made the call to WLVH, it had burst into flames that had sent it to its eternal, well-deserved rest in that big junkyard in the sky.

Yes, she had to win. Though she might yearn to walk away from the contest, the allure of winning the truck was too strong. She needed a vehicle.

She glanced at Judy, who was interviewing Mary's rival for the Chevy. The man was tall and dark-haired. He was wearing jeans — tight jeans that showed off a supremely sculpted backside.

Backside?

Mary Rosenthal wasn't the type of woman who ogled a man's body parts. Now Gilda, her mother, might, but not Mary.

Never Mary.

She was the quiet one, the grounded one. She was the one who'd never ogle a man. But this man . . . well, she figured he was worth a tiny ogle or two.

Mary cut off the very un-Mary-like thoughts. She had to be careful that the novelty of living in a truck didn't tilt her normal world any more than necessary.

But it was a nice backside, and if she was her mother she would definitely notice it and probably even do something about it, she thought idly. Abruptly she pulled her gaze upward and it stuck on the T-shirt that emphasized an equally nice upper body. Well-defined muscles corded his arms; very nicely shaped arms with very nice biceps.

Slowly Mary's gaze rose to his face. Her mouth went dry. Ah, who was she kidding, he was more than nice. He was drop-dead-pick-your-tongue-up-from-the-floor kind of gorgeous.

She'd thought that Punch should leave radio for a place in front of a camera, but his good looks paled next to those of the man who would be playing lead in her fantasies for years to come; the man who she was going to be locked in a pickup with for who knew how long.

Life was so unfair.

"Mary?" The tone of Punch's voice suggested she was supposed to answer something, but she didn't have a clue what.

"Pardon?"

"I said, how do you plan to amuse yourself in our Chevy pickup?"

Amuse herself? Well, she could always daydream about the hunk who was going to be in it with her. She shook her head and tried to clear her man-maddened mind.

That man was definitely off-limits.

Mary hadn't roomed with anyone since her senior year in college and she liked it

20

that way. She liked having things done her way; liked having the quiet solitude of her own place. If she could barely stand a room-mate in college, how was she going to handle sharing the microscopic space the truck would allow with a strange, albeit gor-geous, man? A dorm room certainly offered a lot more living space than a truck — even if it was a full-sized version. They would be lucky if they could get along at all without her messing up the situation with her fantasies. Her cheeks grew warm.

"Read," she blurted.

"Read?"

"Yes. As a teacher, I know the importance of reading and it's how I planned to spend my summer before this contest. During the school year I just don't have enough time to read as much as I'd like. As far as I'm concerned, being in a pickup doesn't change my plans at all. I'm going to work my way through my to-be-read pile."

"Oh." Punch sounded disappointed.

Disappointed, that's how Ethan felt too.

He'd hoped for some flighty little college girl who would miss her dorm parties within a few days and hit the road. His competi-tion had to quit, because his father had decided the Chevy that Ethan didn't need would be the perfect delivery vehicle.

He'd already talked to a local body shop about having the Westbrook Pharmacy logo painted on the sides.

And as much as it pained him to admit it, Ethan had decided his father was right. He still wasn't pleased about living in a truck, but the pharmacies were his responsibility. He hadn't asked for it, but the family's and the business's welfare had settled squarely on Ethan's shoulders.

So, he was stuck in the truck until the woman bailed.

He glanced at his non-flighty adversary who was being interviewed across the room. No, she didn't look like a party animal.

She was average height — well, maybe a little less than average — average weight, and her dark brown hair hung a little ways down her back in a ponytail.

She was wearing sweatpants and a T-shirt that read, "Because I'm the Teacher, that's why." A pair of glasses hung on a chain around her neck and an intimidating stack of books and bags were piled at her Reebok-clad feet.

No, definitely not a party animal. Although despite the fact that all her individual parts looked decidedly average, there was something about her that gave Ethan a slight tug of interest. If they'd been out on the town, he'd have introduced himself to her. He wasn't sure why. Average, comfortable women weren't his style.

Whatever it was tugging at him, he was determined to ignore it. She was his adversary. And despite the fact she looked comfortable in an uncomfortable way, she also looked like a woman planning to dig in her heels and stay in the pickup for as long as it took. Oh, where was a flighty college co-ed when you needed one?

This could turn into an ugly stalemate.

"So, Ethan. What are you doing about your job?" Judy pushed the microphone at him.

"I'm the head of Westbrook Pharmacies here in Erie, Pennsylvania. Westbrook is a family-owned business, and my father offered to come out of retirement and allow me a leave of absence until this contest is over. You see, at Westbrook it's the individual who matters most — whether it's our family, our employees, or our customers, we put their needs first."

"Oh." Judy frowned, obviously not pleased by his blatant advertising. "So, what do you plan to do in the truck?"

"Well, I figure I'll have a lot of time to

catch up on Westbrook Pharmacy's paperwork."

Using the pharmacy's name should make his father happy. Ethan planned to make himself happy by planning a dozen glorious ways to make his father pay for guilting him into this stupid contest.

"Well, I see Punch is motioning to the clock." Judy had obviously decided it was time to end the interview. "It's almost nine. Let's go over the rules one more time. You'll both get fifteen minute restroom breaks throughout the day, and one two hour break in the evening. Other than that, you're in the truck and the first one out loses. The winner gets the brand new Chevy truck, courtesy of Big Al's Auto and WLVH Lovehandles, where love is more than just a song. Now, time to get in." She maneuvered Ethan toward the maroon Chevy that was going to be his home for an indeterminate amount of time.

"Ethan, this is Mary. Mary, Ethan," Judy said, introducing them.

Ethan nodded at his competition and tried to appear as intimidating as possible.

Mary nodded back, apparently oblivious to his tactics.

With a hand in the small of her back, Punch pushed Mary closer to Ethan. "Well, here we go. I'm flipping a coin to see who gets the driver's seat first. Mary, you call it."

"Heads."

Her voice seemed deep for a woman. Deep and husky. The kind of voice that could attract and hold a man's attention. The kind of voice that painted pictures in Ethan's head — pictures that had no business being there.

This Mary wasn't his type.

"Tails it is." Punch's call pulled Ethan from his fantasies — fantasies he knew he couldn't afford to indulge. "Looks like you're in the driver's seat. For now at least."

"For now." Ethan picked up his duffle bag and briefcase and opened the driver's door.

Punch helped Mary move her load of supplies to the passenger side of the pickup in the small space behind the seat.

The maroon Chevy stood on a platform in a glassed-in bay window of Al's showroom, exposed on three out of four sides. The cars that drove down Parade Street had a front row seat for Mary and Ethan's stand off.

Nothing like living in a fishbowl, Ethan thought glumly.

"Here we go. Why doesn't everyone count along with me?" Punch gestured wildly to

25

the crowd that had gathered. "Ten, nine, eight, seven, six, five, four, three, two, one. Inside you go!"

Grimly Ethan crawled into the driver's seat and watched as Mary gave a little hop off the running board and into the seat next to his.

In an unintentional synchronized movement, they slammed the doors. In Ethan's mind it was the sound of a guillotine blade dropping.

Mary ignored the hoopla going on in the showroom and concentrated on the unhappy looking man who was, as of this moment, her pickup buddy.

"Ethan, I hope . . ." Mary's voice trailed off as she studied the determined look on his face. She hoped he'd give up tomorrow and get out of the truck so she could start her vacation.

Oh, she could read in the Chevy as easily as on the beach, but Presque Isle's beaches were a lot more scenic than the car dealer's showroom, and the sun was so much more appealing than the showroom's fluorescent lights.

She couldn't say that though, so she settled for, "I hope, even though we're competing against each other, we can get along."

"Sure," Ethan said with a shrug.

"Is there anything you want me to know? Anything I can do to make this easier on you?" Not that she wanted to make it too easy. She needed this vehicle and it wouldn't do to forget it.

"Yeah, you can get tired of this whole thing and get out as soon as possible."

Her smile faded at the hostility in his voice.

Ethan Westbrook might fill out his well-worn jeans quite nicely, might even be a hunk, but he wasn't very nice. Looks meant nothing to Mary if the person wasn't equally attractive on the inside.

"I can't do that," she said softly.

Mary wasn't about to explain her desperation to this surly man. She didn't want his pity, didn't want any favors. She just wanted — *needed,* she corrected — to win the truck. "But, I will try to stay out of your way, at least as much as I can while we're both sharing the front seat of a pickup. Of course I wouldn't complain if you wanted to climb out and surrender any time soon. I'd hoped to spend the summer at the beach."

She offered him a small, hopeful smile.

In her mind's eye she could see a beautiful Presque Isle sunset fading on the horizon. Regret tugged at her. The peninsula that jutted into Lake Erie boasted the most beautiful beaches around. Sailboats, sunsets, and ice cream — life didn't get any better than that.

But it did get worse. And sharing a maroon Chevy with an ill-natured man qualified as a lot worse.

"Sorry, no can do." Ethan's tone was flat and final.

Mary's dream of the beach popped like a balloon. "Well, then." She shifted in her seat. It looked like she had better get comfortable, since Ethan obviously wasn't going to make this easy.

"Yeah, well then," he echoed.

Their eyes met and for a fraction of a second Mary thought she saw something like regret flicker in Ethan's gray eyes. A moment later it was gone and all that remained was stark determination.

She broke the disturbing contact and looked out her window.

It was going to be a long contest.

It was going to be impossible, Ethan thought as he shifted in his seat. The jeans he'd chosen to wear had seemed comfortable enough when he put them on, but he was beginning to suspect they weren't going to remain comfortable for long when he was spending most of his day sitting in the truck.

Unconsciously he ran his hand over the leather seats. Big Al's and Lovehandles hadn't been stingy. The maroon Chevy was brand new and had that new car smell that any red-blooded American male loved. The dash and door panels were wood-grained and spoke of the extra attention to detail that likened a mode of transportation to a work of art.

Ethan tugged his gray T-shirt, emblazoned with Westbrook Pharmacies, out of his jeans, trying to get more comfortable.

Charles had given him fourteen similar shirts in various colors and styles. Ethan was praying he wouldn't have a chance to wear them all. He wanted this contest finished. He glanced at his opponent. She had stashed her stuff in the back jumpseat and was already buried in one of her books.

She looked totally comfortable. Her sweats seemed like a wise idea. The thick book that proclaimed she was here for the duration seemed wise too. She looked as if she had made herself at home, curled up with her nose buried in the books' pages. Ethan was already tired of the paperwork he'd brought along, and it had only been a half a day.

The crowd had thinned considerably, so there wasn't even anyone left to entertain him, though cars that passed the dealership honked and the radio station's crew was positioned right outside the huge bay window.

He'd talked to dozens of strangers and had managed to plug the pharmacies to each and every one. Seeing how often he could mention them had almost become a game.

His father would be happy.

That made one of them at least.

Mary interrupted his dour thoughts. "You can turn on the radio. If you'd like to, that is."

Ethan wanted to say no thanks. She might be offering because she wanted to listen herself and he certainly didn't want to do anything that would make her more comfortable. But he was bored already, and the radio sounded good.

"We'll drain the battery," he muttered gloomily, even as he turned the key toward him and started flipping the radio buttons.

She smiled. "It's not like we're going anywhere soon." She laughed then; a soft, sensual sound. Not all shrilly like some women and not giggly like the majority of the rest. It was a simple quiet sound that made him want to chuckle as well.

But, he didn't. He wouldn't let himself.

He wasn't going to make friends with the enemy; no matter how nice she seemed, no matter how friendly or accommodating. No matter how desirable.

Desirable?

No. He glanced her way to be sure. No. Ordinary. Not strikingly beautiful. Not desirable. The enemy. She was the only thing standing between him and freedom. It wouldn't do to forget that.

His eyes narrowed and he studied Mary. She definitely didn't look like the type that listened to rock. Other than listening to Lovehandles, she probably went for classical stuff. Hard rock would probably make her crazy.

"Fine," he said. He hit the button with more force than was necessary. Instead of turning to WLVH — a station he'd decided to boycott the moment he *won* the contest — he tuned the dial to the local hard rock station. "You don't mind, do you?"

She looked up from her book, a distracted air about her. "Oh, no, not at all. Gilda, that's my mother, well, she practically weaned me on rock."

"Oh." The single-syllable response was the

best that Ethan could manage.

"If you're bored, you're welcome to borrow a book," she offered. "I brought plenty."

"I haven't read a book since college." And he'd only read then because he had to. He preferred doing things over reading about them.

Mary just smiled. "It might be a good time to cultivate the habit."

That serene little smile was starting to annoy him. No matter what he said or did, she smiled. She smiled at the radio people, at the crowds that had visited them that morning . . . at everyone.

Her nothing-can-bother-me smile seemed to be a permanent part of her features. Being that serene wasn't normal, and Ethan didn't like her tranquil expression one bit.

"No thanks," he practically growled. "If I get desperate, I'll let you know."

He couldn't imagine being desperate enough to read for fun — or foolish enough to fall for her husky voice and sweet smile.

"You do that." She turned back to the book, seemingly shutting out the world around her, including Ethan and the radio which was beating some hard rock song.

Ethan stared at her blatantly and cursed his luck. He wanted to shake her out of her good mood. He wanted her to be as disgruntled as he felt.

Sitting there in her oh-so-comfortable sweats, her small upturned nose buried in the thick book, Mary Rosenthal looked the picture of comfort and contentment. She looked like she could easily spend the entire summer in that very position.

What was she reading anyway? It must be good if her speed in flipping pages was any indication.

Not that he cared.

A bookworm, that's what she was. Not his type.

Before his mind could latch on to another thought regarding her desirability, he reminded himself sternly that she was the enemy.

And his enemy was looking quite settled and pleased with herself.

So much for a quick contest.

DAY THREE

He was staring at her again.

Mary tried to ignore Ethan as she talked to Punch and Judy on the cell phone, but ignoring him was getting harder and harder.

He'd spent the better part of their first two days in the pickup staring at her, and it appeared he was going to spend their third day doing it again.

She toyed with the glasses that dangled from a chain around her neck and answered Punch's question. "No, Ethan's in the driver's seat again today."

"Now, that's the way the world should be run," Punch said. His obnoxious behavior seemed to be part of his radio trademark. "The guy in the driver's seat."

Judy's voice followed on his heels. "You and I know that women are as capable, and frequently more capable, than men. And, you'll notice it's Mary taking our phone call this morning, not Ethan."

"Yeah, it's one of the things women excel at — talking on the phone."

There was a strangled growl from Judy.

Mary laughed. She enjoyed Punch and Judy's on-air sparks. She wondered if his radio persona was real or just for show. At least some of it had to be put on. At least she hoped some of it was an act.

Punch continued, "So, Mary, any sparks flying between you and your opponent? I mean, a man and a woman stuck together in a car . . . something's bound to happen."

Mary felt her cheeks heat up, but beat back the embarrassment. She took a deep calming breath as she replied, "No, the only thing happening here is the car lot. I can't believe how many people stopped in yesterday to check out Al's bargains. I hope even more come to visit today."

The more people visited, the less time she had to worry about her surly carmate.

There was also the added benefit to mentioning the car dealership. She liked Big Al, the elderly pot-bellied man who had introduced himself the first day and was co-sponsor of the contest. Mary had decided she'd get a plug in for him whenever she could. Ethan certainly was plugging his pharmacies and Al deserved equal time.

Punch totally ignored her pitch. "No

chemistry yet?" There was hope in his voice.

"No chemistry yet — no chemistry ever," she assured him as calmly as she could.

She glanced at Ethan who was staring out his window. Was he listening, or was he really as distracted by something outside the truck as he appeared to be?

She didn't like thinking of chemistry and Ethan. The two words seemed to fit together a little too easily and chemistry wasn't her strongest subject. It had been the only class in school where she'd gotten below average grades. Unfortunately real life seemed to follow suit.

Punch heaved an audible sigh. "So what are the two of you doing in there?"

"Well, so far I've read four books." Four romances in which the heroes all seemed to resemble Ethan Westbrook. "And Ethan's done some paperwork, listened to the radio, and watched some sport thing on this tiny little television he has plugged into the cigarette lighter. Al's mechanics hooked up the battery to a charger, so we don't have to worry about running it down. Big Al's the best. If I wasn't going to win this truck, I'd be buying a car from him."

Ethan turned and shot her a glance, then returned to staring out the window. So he was listening. What was he thinking? His look hadn't told her a thing.

Well, she wasn't going to waste any time thinking about it. She'd decided yesterday when she asked Al about a generator that Ethan didn't react like a normal person. Rather than acting grateful, or even relieved, Ethan had acted annoyed.

Mary simply couldn't figure the man out. He glared at her and got annoyed over the littlest things, like when she'd agreed to listen to the music he chose, and when she talked to Al about the generator. She was just trying to get along, but he didn't seem interested in making the best of a bad situation. Well that was fine with her.

"Thinking about throwing in the towel yet?" The cell phone's reception was a bit fuzzy, but Mary could just make out Judy's question.

"Oh, no. I'm here to win," Mary said it with all the conviction she could muster. Ethan faced her again and his glare intensified — not that Mary cared.

She had to win. Losing wasn't an option. Oh, Ethan didn't show any signs of giving up, but he was going to have to, because Mary couldn't. If only she could convince him to give up sooner, rather than at the end of her vacation.

"And on that note, let's hear from Al's

Auto." Judy segued into a commercial. "Okay, we're off the air now. Anything you guys need down there?"

"No, but thanks. With a charger on the battery, we're really quite comfortable, considering the circumstances. The restaurant next door, The Blarney Scone, has been bringing over the most delicious meals. I'm going to waddle when I finally get out of this truck."

"Okay, the commercial's almost over. Call you later." Judy hung up.

Mary was left holding the phone.

"You can take the next call," she said to her quiet carmate.

"Fine."

Ethan wasn't just a man of few words, he was pretty much a man of no words. There was the occasional grunt and once he'd slipped and hummed along with a song, but other than that he remained silent. Staring and glaring seemed to be his two primary means of communication.

"Look, if you hate being here so much, why don't you just open the door and get out?" Mary realized it wasn't the most tactfully phrased suggestion, but she didn't apologize.

"I can't." His mouth hardened into a grim line.

She wondered if the man had a pleasant bone in his entire body.

She felt as grim as he looked, but she grinned a grin that she knew didn't go any further than her mouth just to prove she could. "Sure you can. Just pull the little handle and, voila, you're free."

"I can't. This is good publicity for the pharmacies. Too good for me to leave. Why are you here?"

This was the closest they'd come to conversing since they had entered the stupid truck. It wasn't that she wanted to know the man, she was simply bored. The people who stopped by to say hi looked at them as if they were animals at the zoo.

Mary just wanted a conversation. She didn't have to like Ethan Westbrook in order to talk to him.

She considered his question.

Why *was* she here? She might want to talk to him, but she didn't feel the need to tell him everything about herself.

"I'm here until the end," she finally replied.

"But why?"

"Because I've always wanted a pickup truck. With Erie's winter storms, the four-wheel drive is perfect."

And because I need it, she added silently.

"You haven't won yet," he reminded her, his tone suggesting she wasn't going to. "So, why don't you get out and go talk to Al. I'll bet he'd give you a deal. You were certainly sweet-talking him enough last night."

"Have you ever seen a teacher's pay stub?" she asked abruptly.

He shook his head.

"Well, you'd need a magnifying glass to read the numbers because they're so small. So small in fact that after I pay my bills and my student loans every month, there's not enough left for something like this."

She didn't add that buying any car at all, no matter how inexpensive, was equally out of the question.

"If teaching pays so poorly, why do it?"

Could that be real interest in his voice?

She stared at him a minute, wishing she could read his mind, but she couldn't tell for sure. His question hadn't thrown her at all because she'd asked herself the same one on countless occasions.

"Because I love it. I get up in the morning looking forward to my day. Because every day is an adventure and, when all is said and done, money isn't everything."

The first part was a truth she'd recognized early on, but the last part, the part about money not being everything, was something she had to remind herself of frequently.

Very frequently since her Pinto had died.

"Money's not everything, unless you have none and want a brand new pickup?" His tone didn't sound sarcastic. As a matter of fact, it sounded like amusement.

After two days of scowls, Mary was taking anything she could get, even questionable humor.

She grinned. "Something like that."

For half a second it looked as though Ethan might smile as well, but the tug at the corner of his lips was so quick, Mary couldn't be sure she saw it.

When she looked again there was no smile on his face, not even a hint of one. She decided she must have imagined it.

He studied her with that stone-faced expression and said, "I guess we have a problem then."

"What problem? You can always leave," she said with more hope in her voice than she actually felt.

"It sounds like neither of us is planning to leave anytime soon." Determination laced his voice.

Mary's heart sank.

"You're sure you won't reconsider?" she asked, though she didn't hold out much hope.

41

"No. You?"

All dreams of a quiet summer on the beach faded.

"Sorry, I can't," she said with a great deal of regret.

Obviously her response didn't please him because Ethan turned and faced out the window again.

That was okay with her. At least he wasn't staring at her. She didn't need to talk to him — she had more reading to keep her busy. She picked up a new JoAnn Ross book and dug in. A story of everlasting love was enough to sweep her thoughts away from Ethan, the pickup, and a beachless summer.

Ethan watched some lame soap opera on his tiny, hand-held television. As he tried to make out the tiny shapes, he found himself wishing for his television at home; a huge beauty of a television. When he watched a baseball game he almost believed he could reach out and grab the ball.

He would have sighed, but he didn't want to give *her* any clue that he was finding their confinement difficult.

She sat comfortably, nose in a book, looking for all intents and purposes as if she could stay in the pickup all summer.

All summer? The thought was more depressing than watching soap operas on a microscopic screen.

He had season tickets for the Braves. He had women to date, buddies to hang with and . . . well, he had stuff to do. A great deal of important stuff and Miss Bookworm was ruining it all.

"Ethan."

He jumped, startled by his friend's voice at his window.

Now Barney was someone who wouldn't mind living in a truck, and yet there he was, walking around and enjoying the summer. The situation wasn't fair.

"Barney. Aren't you supposed to be working?"

Ethan knew he was being juvenile. It wasn't Barney's fault he was stuck in the cramped cab of the Chevy, after all.

"Good to see you," he added as an apology.

Barney was never one to take offense. "Your dad's changed the schedule around a bit. How goes it?"

His father was messing with his schedule? Ethan bit back his annoyance. "Well, Barn, I've had more fun."

Barney grinned that cockeyed grin of his. "Rick's bachelor party last week for instance?"

Ethan grimaced. "That wasn't fun — that was torture. I'm too old to party like that."

He used to spend entire weekends partying, but somehow, two beers into the evening, Ethan had been ready to call it a night. He'd only stayed because . . . he had no idea why he'd stayed. Maybe just to prove he wasn't getting too old, to prove that the lifestyle he'd enjoyed since college was still a good one.

Barney laughed like Ethan's admission was some joke. "I'm not too old for parties like that and since we're the same age, you can't be either."

Not wanting to talk about how old he was feeling, Ethan went back to the subject of his father. "So what else is going on at the stores? What's my father done, other than switch the schedules around?"

"It's quiet without you. And, he's not doing so bad, except when he has to go near the computer. He's taken to calling it names. 'Spawn of Satan' is the latest."

Ethan laughed. His dad wasn't a very technologically advanced soul.

Ethan leaned on the window, suddenly more relaxed. Joking and laughing with Barney made it seem as if everything was normal — as if his legs weren't beginning to cramp from sitting so long. As if he

44

wasn't trapped by his father and by his responsibility to the stores.

It was Ethan's laughter that pulled Mary out of her book. She'd been right — a smiling, laughing Ethan Westbrook was a beautiful sight to behold.

"So, introduce me to the babe," Ethan's friend said as he gave Mary the once over.

"Babe?" Genuine confusion laced Ethan's voice.

"Your pickup-mate," the man said.

"Oh." Ethan's brows drew together. He looked at Mary as if he'd never seen her before.

Mary should have been insulted, but she knew she wasn't a *babe* and couldn't be annoyed that Ethan didn't think so either.

Okay, she couldn't be *very* annoyed.

Ethan leaned back in the seat so she could get a good look at his friend. He offered no hint of a smile. "Barney, this is Mary. Mary, Barney."

"You work at the pharmacy too?" she asked.

"Sure do. The E-man and I met at college — frat brothers. When we graduated, he suggested I apply at his dad's stores and, remembering how much fun we had in school, I couldn't resist. Although, he was a

45

lot more fun before he started running things."

"Ethan was fun?"

She had a hard time picturing the mono-syllabic grump as fun. Obviously her doubts came through in her inflection because Ethan didn't look very impressed by her question.

But it would take more than a dig at Ethan to ruin Barney's good mood. He had the look of someone who thought life was all one big joke and didn't seem to mind her asking.

He reached to pat Ethan's back. "Ethan's the life of the party. You must be the only female over the age of eighteen in the city of Erie who doesn't think so. Let me tell you, he always had a gorgeous babe on his arm."

She shrugged. "Guess I'll take your word for it."

Ethan cast her one more frown and then leaned forward, blocking her view out his window and deliberately cutting off her conversation with his friend.

Mary picked up her book, but didn't get to open it. Two men were at her window.

"Hi," the dark-haired one said.

She sighed. She was much better with children than with adults. And much better with women than with men. She just didn't understand the gender, and Ethan was a prime example of her inability to comprehend them.

She conversed with her two visitors, answered their questions, and tried to ignore Ethan and Barney, though it was difficult. Ethan's every chuckle made her pulse speed up just a little more.

She wasn't sure why.

Day Four

"Mary," a man's voice called.

Not just any man, she realized. Ethan. Ethan was calling her.

Mary smiled and opened her arms, arms that were soon filled with a man — more specifically Ethan Westbrook.

"Mary, I've wanted to hold you for so long," he confessed, his voice, a husky whisper, sending ripples of desire inching up her spine.

"Oh, Ethan."

Oh, Ethan? That didn't sound like something she'd say, especially not in that breathless little voice. She wasn't a sigh-over-a-man sort of girl. She was strong. She was sensible. She stood on her own two feet.

"Mary," Ethan said again, his voice more insistent.

"Ethan," she muttered, "be quiet, I'm sleeping."

She snuggled into her pillow and tried to

48

recapture the feel of those strong arms wrapped around her.

Almost afraid to open her eyes, Mary cracked one lid. Instead of seeing part of the maroon chevy or its leather interior, she saw blue . . . the same shade of blue that jeans were made of.

She opened her eye a little wider.

She was definitely looking at denim.

Denim with a flash of gold.

Denim and a zipper.

Mary sat up with a jerk.

Embarrassment flooded her body, wiping out any remaining feelings from her dream.

"I'm so sorry."

She wasn't sure if she was apologizing for dreaming about him, or for using him as a pillow.

She'd been sleeping with her head in Ethan's lap. The thought embarrassed her even more.

Heat tingled in her cheeks. "I didn't mean . . . Well, I mean, I certainly wouldn't intentionally put my face . . . well, there," she finished lamely.

"It's okay Mary. I could have moved you if I'd wanted." Though his lips were up-turned, it wasn't quite a smile. It was the kind of look men saved for women much different than Mary, women they might

49

dream about as well.

"You're saying you wanted me to lay there?" Outrage made her voice quiver. At least she hoped outrage was the feeling she was experiencing right now. It had to be outrage — it couldn't be anything else making her whole body flush and tingle.

"Honey, we might be adversaries, but most men don't object to a lady snuggling close."

"Why you . . ." She searched her thoughts for a good enough name, but drawing a blank, finally just said, *"man."* Of course, she said man in such a way that it was an insult because she was annoyed. More than annoyed. She was outraged that he found the situation funny.

Yes, she was sure that she was experiencing outrage. No sane woman would ever experience desire for a man who annoyed her so regularly.

"I thought you'd like to get up before the employees arrive," he said through a smile. "It might give Punch ideas if he got wind of it."

Sure, *now* he smiled. Her hero.

"You're right, I wouldn't want them to find me with my head on your lap, and I certainly wouldn't want to give Punch any ideas, though I doubt he's very good at thinking hard enough to have an idea," she said in the same quiet voice she used to keep thirty unruly five-year-olds in line.

"So," she continued, "though I appreciate you waking me up, I would have appreciated it more if you'd woke me the second you found my head . . . well, there."

"I'll keep that in mind next time." The confidence in his voice suggested he truly believed there would be a next time.

Well, she would disabuse him of that notion. "There won't *be* a next time." Never. Not in a million years was she going to touch the pig, much less fantasize again about his cute backside —

What had made her think of his butt now? It was the foreside of Ethan that was the problem today, not the aft side.

His grin widened. "Oh, I'm sure —"

What Ethan was sure of Mary would never know. He cut off the sentence as the lights in the showroom flipped on.

Al peeked in Mary's window. "Good morning, sunshine."

Giving Ethan one more glare, she turned and smiled at the elderly gentleman despite her annoyance at Ethan. "Good morning to you, too."

"You look well rested," Al said with paternal concern.

"She slept very well last night."

Ethan, leaning across the seat, peeked out the window from over her shoulder, not quite touching her, but much too close for comfort.

Mary elbowed him as discreetly as possible. At his *groan* of distress, she felt better and smiled with satisfaction before she turned her smile on Al. "I'm ready for my shower. I never truly appreciated my life until it was reduced to the inside of this pickup. Just going to the bathroom is a treat."

Al glanced at his watch. "Well, I'm starting the clock now. You've got an hour."

"Thanks." Mary reached behind her to grab her bag and stiffly got out of the truck. She watched Ethan do the same and was thankful she wasn't as tall as he was. She had more options for positions than he did.

Al was a thoughtful man and had provided two separate facilities at the showroom. Showers for his mechanics even. So there was no toss for who went first. Both Ethan and Mary could enjoy their free hour alone.

Within seconds Mary stood in the shower, unwilling to waste a glorious moment of her freedom or the hot water. She wasn't even going to think about Ethan Westbrook for the entire hour.

Of course she wouldn't.

She didn't like him or care how his butt looked in his jeans. Didn't he know baggier styles were in fashion now?

He probably knew, she thought grumpily, lathering her hair. He probably knew but didn't care. No doubt he wanted to flaunt his stupendous gluteus maximus. He was the kind of man who would enjoy driving women insane.

Not that it bothered Mary Rosenthal. She wasn't interested in him.

He wasn't her type.

She stepped from the stall flushed with heat.

Thank goodness she had this whole sixty minutes away from him. She didn't have to think about him, didn't have to bear looking at his gloriously sculpted body.

This was the best hour of the day. She tossed the towel on a chair and crawled back under the shower head, this time with cold water coursing over her.

She didn't have to think of Ethan at all.

But when she left the restroom she found him waiting outside the door, looking at her and smiling.

"Okay, what's with the smile?"

"What's not to smile about? We're out of the truck."

She allowed a small upturn of her lips in return. "Well, there is that."

"I thought we might take a walk?"

"We can leave the showroom?"

"No. But we could take a few laps around the showroom and stretch our legs. I don't know about you, but I've had enough sitting to last me a long while."

"Me, too," Mary said, studying Ethan. He seemed far too pleasant all of a sudden. She wondered if he was up to something.

He offered her his arm. "Shall we?"

Not knowing what he could be up to, or what she could do about it if she managed to figure it out, Mary simply shrugged and reached toward his arm. "Let's go."

A jolt of something flooded her system as they touched.

Mary refused to analyze what the feeling was. She just enjoyed Ethan's unusual good humor and the brisk walk.

DAY FIVE

"Sky, my love, why didn't you call me? It's times like this that a girl needs her mother's support."

Mary bit back a groan at the sound of the voice.

Day five.

Ever since her walk with Ethan, he'd been more pleasant and she'd felt more optimistic.

That optimism took a decided plunge.

She'd thought she was going to make it through the entire contest without being discovered.

But looking out the window, Mary faced the fact that hope was fleeting and she was indeed discovered. Neon colors assaulted her eyes — colors that seemed at odds with hair so dark the hue could only have come from a bottle. The exotic face framed by the yards of midnight black hair was frowning in worry.

Mary faced the inevitable — her mother had found her. Peace was now a thing of the past.

"How did you find out?" she asked.

With drama worthy of an Oscar, Gilda sniffed. "I was in my car and switching the radio station around when I heard a disc jockey talking about Mary Rosenthal living in a truck. At first I thought you must have lost your apartment and were living in a car. Then I remembered you didn't drive a truck, but that old Pinto."

"It died," Mary said softly.

Gilda went on talking as if Mary hadn't said a thing. "And, then I remembered that little card I filled out for you at the grocery store. A chance to win a truck. I just didn't know you had to live in it to win it. I called the radio station right away and they gave me all the details."

She staged another huge sniff to let the world know how put-upon she was. "I can't believe you didn't call me."

"There was nothing you could have done." Nothing but create a scene. Gilda Rosenthal was very good at scenes. As a matter of fact, she thrived on them. The more dramatic and conspicuous, the better.

"I could have supported you."

Gilda glanced beyond Mary to Ethan.

56

Speculation lit her dark eyes and Mary knew down to the center of her very being what was coming next. The knowledge didn't make her mother's attempted match-making easier to bear.

Mary loved her mother, but Gilda's entire life seemed dedicated to making a scene. Not screaming, hysterical scenes, but look-at-me-I-flaunt-all-the-rules scenes.

Mary read Gilda's expression and knew her mother was about to try and land her a man.

"Who's your truck-mate?" Gilda looked like a cat in front of a saucer of cream.

"Ethan." Mary turned slightly, allowing Gilda and Ethan to see each other fully. "Ethan, this is my mother, Gilda Rosenthal. Gilda, this is Ethan Westbrook."

"My, aren't you a picture? I've been try-ing to get Mary to loosen up and find a man for years. I must say I'm impressed with the one she finally settled on. Living with a man — you've done your mother proud."

She'd known her mother would create a scene, but it didn't lessen her embarrass-ment.

"Mother," she groaned, "I am not *living* with Ethan."

Gilda held up a hand, flashing her neon orange fingernails and ring-ladened fingers.

"Now, Mary, you know I approve. You've needed to break out a bit and let yourself go. Marriage is just an archaic trap for women. All the work, but none of the glory. But living with a hunk? Well, you get all the goodies and none of the headaches. You can walk at any time."

"Actually, I can't walk at any time. Ethan has to be the one to leave because I'm winning this pickup."

"I'm not leaving," Ethan said cheerily from behind her.

"When I said you needed to break out of your routine, I meant date a little, maybe have a wild and passionate fling. But honey! You've surpassed all my expectations. I'm so proud of you."

"I'm not breaking out because if I do break out, I lose."

"Looks like you've already won, from where I'm standing." Gilda quirked her eyebrow and glanced past Mary at Ethan.

"*Some* women would agree with you, Mrs. Rosenthal," Ethan piped up. "They seem to think I'm a good catch."

"I'm sure Mary agrees with them," Gilda said.

"I do *not* agree with all of Ethan's other women. He might think he's a catch, but someone dropped the ball somewhere. All he does is watch television. Soap operas, sports, commercials, it doesn't matter. He's not a good catch — he's a couch potato."

She was running out of steam and a sense of direction to finish her soliloquy. "And my life is just fine, thank you very much."

She finished with a humph and managed not to stick her tongue out like one of her kindergartners would.

"All you've done is read and flirt with the guys who visit," Ethan tossed back.

"I do not flirt." She never flirted and wouldn't even know where to begin.

"How about those three men yesterday?"

"Who?" She didn't have a clue. There had been any number of visitors in the last five days, and after a while they all ran together in her mind.

"You know, while Barney was here?"

"Oh them. They were looking at trucks and wanted to know how I liked this one," she said with all her teacher-like primness.

"And what did you say?" Hope filled Gilda's voice and a glimmer lit her dark eyes.

"I said it was a great vehicle, except for the company. Not that I've actually driven it anywhere. That will come later, *after* I've won."

Gilda winked at Ethan. "I'd say the company looked pretty good from where I'm standing."

"He would appeal to you, Mother. But I want something more than a beer-gulping couch potato when I fall for a man."

She turned and gave Ethan one more sharp look and then positioned herself at the window in such a way that he was cut out of the conversation.

Ethan smirked. Mary obviously didn't want him joining the conversation. Well, that was fine with him. He wasn't interested in uptight Mary "I'm-going-to-win-the-pickup-or-die-trying" Rosenthal.

He peeked at Gilda. Mary's mother? The two women couldn't have looked more different. Gilda was tall with long dark hair she could probably sit on. She wore heavy make-up, tons of jewelry and flowing robes in colors that were almost as loud as she was.

"So. About your hunk?" Gilda asked.

Ethan purposely stared out his own window, pretending he wasn't interested in what the two of them had to say.

No, he wasn't pretending, he *wasn't* interested. He didn't care what Mary thought of him, or what her mother thought, though it was apparent her mother had better taste than she did.

Okay, so maybe Gilda's clothes didn't

quite reflect good taste, but she had a refined sense of what defined a great catch.

He had grown more annoyed at Mary with each passing hour. She never said a word about his choice in television programs, just tilted that perky little nose in disapproval.

No, he didn't care at all what she thought about him.

Oh, they'd gotten along better since she had slept on his lap and the walk around the showroom that followed yesterday. They'd chatted and joked. For a few minutes, he'd felt normal. And some of the feeling lasted even after they'd climbed back in the truck.

They'd taken another walk this morning. It felt as if it could be a ritual, although he was hoping the contest ended long before any of their routines became ritualized.

"Well, Ethan," Gilda called loudly.

Ethan turned, ignoring Mary, and leaning to get a good look at her mother.

"It was nice meeting you. Take good care of my girl. She tries to be a stick in the mud, but if you watch carefully, you'll see she's more fun than you thought. Maybe more fun than she thought."

He did Gilda the courtesy of not laughing in her face and smiled. "I would have thought you were Mary's sister if you hadn't told me different."

"Oh, he's a charmer," Gilda said to Mary.

"Yeah, a charmer alright." Mary glared at him.

"Now, Sky . . ."

"Mary, Mother. It's been Mary since I was ten." She cringed, aware that Ethan was hanging on their every word.

Gilda sighed the sigh of the truly put-upon. "I never did understand why you changed it. Sky's such a nice name, isn't it Ethan?"

"A very nice name," he agreed with a smile. *Sky.* Yes, he liked it. And despite the fact she was again wearing a comfortable looking T-shirt and sweats, he could see a hint of the extraordinary in her. Yes, plain old Mary Rosenthal had a hint of Sky in her. Oh, she buried it, but when you lived with someone for almost a week, you saw things . . . things they might not want you to see.

He saw Sky.

Ethan thought it was funny, Mary realized. She scowled at him.

"I changed it because it didn't fit me and you agreed." She used her best teacher voice and a condescending glare.

"But if you'd worked a little harder it

62

could have fit you. Just think how much more fun you'd have as Sky Blue than as Mary. Mary's so ordinary," her mother insisted.

"I am ordinary. I'm ordinary," Mary repeated again for good measure. Peacefully, blissfully ordinary.

"No you're exceptional."

"Said with a mother's bias."

That was the thing about Gilda, she might be a bit off the beaten trail — okay not just off the trail, she forged her own twisted trail — and she might delight in being the center of attention, but Mary never doubted, not even for a moment, that her mother truly believed that she was exceptional.

Mary had never doubted she was loved.

She moved slightly, trying once again to block Ethan from the conversation.

"You're sure there's nothing you need?" Gilda asked.

"Really, I'm fine." She reached for her mother's hand and gave it a quick squeeze.

Gilda's smile blossomed. "Well, if you think of anything, you just let me know. As long as I'm here, I'm going to look at a car on the back lot. I saw it when I pulled in."

"What kind of car?"

"A Volkswagen van. It reminds me of the car you were conceived in."

"Mother." Her tender feelings turned to annoyance with that one outrageous sentence.

"Sky."

"Mary," she reminded her mother again.

Gilda shook her head in disgust, but her smile gave her away. "Stubborn. You were always so very stubborn."

"Go look at your car, Mother. Al's a very nice man. I bet he'll give you a deal."

"Well, I'll stop and say good-bye when I leave. And you know if you need money . . ."

Mary cut off the offer. "I'm fine, Mother. Good-bye."

"I'll be in to see you every day, now that I know you're here."

"I can't wait." Mary watched her mother hurry purposefully away and smothered a groan.

"Sky?" Ethan raised an amused brow.

"Not one word. Not one." If she murdered him and booted the body out of the pickup, would she still win the contest? she wondered.

"Sky?" he repeated.

The idea had merit, she thought grimly.

Mary was getting to know Ethan well enough to realize he wasn't going to let it go. He almost appeared to be enjoying her discomfort. Maybe she was too sensitive

64

around him? Maybe, just maybe, he was kidding her?

She must be wrong. Ethan Westbrook didn't like her and he wouldn't joke with her as if she were a friend.

"My mother named me Sky Blue because she said my eyes were the oddest shade of blue she'd ever seen. When I was ten, I had it changed legally. I mean, Sky Blue? Do I look like a Sky Blue?"

"Well." His brows drew together as if he were considering the question seriously. "Lean over."

"What?"

"Lean over so I can see your eyes." He circled her forearm and gave a little pull. Mary leaned, staring into Ethan's gray eyes as he stared into hers. "I think your mother might have had a point."

His voice was soft, a feathery whisper she could feel brush her cheek.

Mary's heart did a little flip. If another man had said it, she would have thought that he was flirting with her, but Ethan wouldn't flirt with her. He didn't even like her.

"Thank you. I guess." She tried to draw her eyes away from his, but she was caught in his gaze. "I —" She couldn't think of anything to say.

"So why Mary?" he asked, not backing off at all, not releasing her arm.

Mary pulled free and slid back in the seat, trying to create some space between them — at least as much space as the tight confines of the cab would allow.

Ethan might have let her arm go, but he held her gaze with his own.

"I . . ." She tried to form a rational thought. "I named myself after my grandmother. She was a decidedly normal lady and that's all I ever wanted to be. Normal. Just one of the gang. Someone who could fade into the woodwork."

"A Mary can be normal, but a Sky Blue can't?"

"Living with Gilda was abnormal enough. I did everything I could to tilt the scales toward the regular."

"Regular isn't always what it's cracked up to be."

"Ethan!" A loud boisterous voice interrupted whatever he was going to say next.

"Dad?"

This time it was Mary who was fascinated. She slid closer, trying to get a good look at the man — the man who Ethan claimed was forcing him into staying in her truck.

A more mature copy of Ethan peered into the interior and shrugged. "I meant to make it down here sooner, but things are crazy at the pharmacy. You put everything on computer." It was an obvious accusation.

Ethan's shoulders tensed. "We talked about it before I did it. By computerizing the business, and linking all four stores into one system, we've eliminated —"

His father shrugged. "All I hear is yada, yada, yada, which is pretty much my understanding of the computer system."

"Dad, it's designed to be user-friendly. Even Barney gets it."

"Barney?" His father grimaced.

"Barney. As a matter of fact, you might want to ask him to show you the ropes."

"Ask Barney? The same Barney Clark that you often refer to as Barney Fife?"

"One and the same." The tension in Ethan's back eased. He was enjoying himself. Mary would have known it even if she hadn't spent the last five days confined with him in the close confines of the pickup.

"You're just doing this to humiliate me?" There was a challenge in his father's stance.

"And you think asking Barney for help is more humiliating than living in a truck?" Ethan's back stiffened again.

His father ignored Ethan's annoyance and looked at Mary. "I might not have been down here, but I've been listening on the

67

radio. You must be Mary."

"Mary this is my father. Mary Rosenthal, Charles Westbrook."

"Pleased to meet you, sir." The man seemed to share a lot of the same mannerisms with his son. They both seemed determined to have their own way. Under other circumstances she might feel sympathy for Ethan — she knew what it was like to live with an overbearing parent.

She leaned forward and offered Charles a small smile and her hand. Her elbow brushed Ethan's chest and Mary managed to ignore the way her heart raced with the contact, but she couldn't ignore the way he smelled. It was a battle every morning not to bury her nose in his neck and savor the smell of him.

Touching him, smelling him — this was getting out of hand.

Charles' firm hand shake forced her back to reality with a thud.

"Nice to meet you. I've been waiting a long time for this boy to get off his duff and find a woman. You're the first one he's lived with."

"Dad," Ethan groaned and ran a hand down his clean-shaven cheek.

Charles ignored him. "Is he a good roommate? I mean, I'd like to know if we have a chance of ever getting another woman to live with him."

"He's okay, I guess, as far as roommates go. The last roommate I had was in college and she had a revolving door on the room. Men, coming and going at all hours. Ethan's not like that, thank goodness."

Enjoying Ethan's discomfort wasn't nice, but Mary had never claimed to be overly nice. They both might have domineering parents, but he was still the enemy and she couldn't afford to empathize.

"Ethan does have a revolving door, just not on the pickup, I suppose. I wish he would just settle on one." There was a wistful note in the man's voice.

The thought of Ethan having a steady march of women in his life didn't set well, though it clearly didn't matter to her. Ethan might occasionally serve as a good pillow, but nothing more. His father's comment only added to Mary's conviction on that point.

She forced a smile. "Well, don't give up, Mr. Rosenthal. He's got a lot of potential."

"He does?"

"Certainly. I've dated enough losers to recognize potential in one when I see it."

"Okay, you two. Enough talking about me as if I wasn't here." Ethan glared at her.

"Fine. You two enjoy your conversation," Mary turned to talk to the people who had gathered at her window.

Mary was talking to another group of spectators. A male group.

Every time Ethan turned around there were men at her window. Mary wasn't fashion-model gorgeous, but there was a genuine beauty in her. A beauty that obviously shone over the radio waves. She had a quickly growing fan club.

Even Big Al had become a member.

Ethan didn't like all her groupies. It wasn't that he was interested in her himself. It was just that he felt responsible for her. She seemed so guileless about men and he didn't like the idea of anyone taking advantage of her.

No matter what his father said, Ethan wasn't looking for a woman.

He liked his life. He worked hard, and when he was done at the office he wanted to relax. Women weren't relaxing.

Baseball was relaxing.

His buddies were relaxing.

Even doing his laundry had a certain rhythm to it which could be relaxing.

But women weren't relaxing.

Not ever.

Women were demanding. They were always insisting that a man notice their clothes, their hair, every little thing. Not that Mary expected any of that, but then she didn't count. She was probably equally as demanding with men she was involved with.

Of course, he dated, but he made it a habit of never dating anyone for long. Women tended to see consecutive dates as some sort of commitment, and Ethan didn't want that.

Women wanted a man to account for every hour of the day. They didn't understand how important baseball was. He just didn't get them. Maybe it was because he had lost his mother when he was seven and it had been just him and his dad.

Oh, there was Aunt Constance, but she did little to recommend the female species. She had totally browbeat her own husband until the day he passed away. Ethan always thought Uncle Audin's death had been a form of self-preservation.

What Mary did was her own business, but Ethan felt responsible because she was, for the time being, his truck-mate. It wasn't that he'd noticed that she had that cute little way of twirling her hair as she read. It was a turn-on, he had to admit.

Not that he was turned on. Another man

might be, but not him.

Okay, there were her glasses too. Glasses shouldn't be a turn-on.

Never before had a woman in a pair of glasses affected his libido, but this woman . . . When she slipped on those glasses and picked up a book, Ethan wanted to kiss her senseless.

And when she didn't have the glasses on her face, she twirled them absentmindedly, but there was nothing absent in the way the habit affected Ethan.

His desire couldn't have anything to do with who she was — it had to be the mere fact that she was a woman. She was a woman who had spent hours sleeping in his lap — hours that he hadn't slept a wink.

"Ethan," Charles barked.

"Hm?"

"I asked, how much longer are you going to be stuck here? I miss the golf course."

Hope crept into Ethan's voice. "Say the word. I'd be happy to open the door and get out right now."

Charles shook his head. "You can't do that. We're five days closer to winning."

He dropped his voice and leaned closer. "No, you can't be the one to get out. I just want to know how close the girl is to quitting. She seems nice enough, but she should

72

really just give up since you've told her you're not going to. You *have* told her?"

"Again and again. But as far as I can tell she's here for the long haul. She brought a bag of books. I've never seen anything like it. She picks one up and disappears somewhere. I don't think she cares where she is as long as she has books."

"Is there any way we can keep her from having them?" Charles whispered.

"Are you planning a book-napping?"

Charles frowned. "I guess not."

"Well, then that's that. I'm here until she leaves and, from what I can tell, that won't be until school starts."

"You mean you're here for the summer?"

"Unless something changes."

Charles looked even more depressed than Ethan felt.

Part of Ethan was glad his father wasn't enjoying himself. It was only fair. Oh, being with Mary wasn't all that difficult, but it couldn't compare to his season tickets to watch the Cleveland Indians play.

"Guess I'd better get Barney to show me the basics of this new computer system then."

His father's misery suited Ethan just fine. After all, if he had to spend the summer in a pickup, Charles should have to suffer too.

And not golfing seemed to be inflicting huge amounts of pain.

The thought cheered Ethan immeasurably. "Well, have fun," he said.

"Sure. I'm trading my nine iron in for a mouse. Lots of fun there. Do you need anything?"

Was that a hint of paternal concern?

"No, I'm fine."

"Well, call me if you do. I'll bring it down or send someone with it."

"Fine."

Charles left Ethan alone with his thoughts. And as he listened to Mary laughing over something Tweedledee, Tweedledum and Tweedle-dumber said, his thoughts weren't all that pleased.

His little goldfish was swimming with piranha.

Al's had closed. Mary and Ethan had enjoyed a nice long out-of-the-truck break. When Al said it was time to get back in, every fiber of Mary's being screamed against it. "We could call it a draw," she said to Ethan. "We could just turn around, walk out of here and get on with our lives."

It was tempting. Tantalizing even.

"I wish we could," Ethan sighed. "But I can't. I wouldn't complain if you stayed out though."

"No," she said glumly.

"Let's go," Al said.

They both climbed into the cab.

Mary was sick of reading, sick of being cramped. She wanted a day-long bubble bath and she wanted to sleep in a real bed, all stretched out and nestled on a pile of pillows.

She wanted to be miles away from Ethan Westbrook and his stupid little television; a television he never offered to share.

"Mary."

She jumped at the sound. Since the store had closed down, neither of them had said a word.

"What?" she asked suspiciously. Ethan's voice sounded almost pleasant.

A pleasant Ethan was still a scary thing. She could like a pleasant Ethan, and Mary didn't want to like her competitor.

"Remember you offered to let me borrow a book? Does the offer still stand?"

She must be hearing things. She was getting antsier than she thought. He looked serious though. "You want to borrow a book?"

"I'm sick of television and the radio. You seem taken with them, so I thought I'd give one a try, if you're still willing to share."

75

"I brought mainly romance."

She read a little of this and a little of that, but for pleasure she mainly stuck to romance. She loved the character development and watching relationships flourish despite all the adversity the authors threw at them.

Ethan groaned. "Romance?"

Mary was quick to jump to her favorite genre's defense. "Hey, don't say it like that. A lot of guys read romance."

"Name one," Ethan challenged.

Without a thought, Mary had an answer. "My friend Sarah's dad does."

"What is he, a hairdresser?"

He was joking, but Mary wasn't laughing. "No, Sarah and her dad are both contractors. Don't tell me Ethan Westbrook is so worried about his masculinity that he won't dare read a romance?"

The dig must have worked because his face flushed.

"Just pick one out and give it to me," he growled.

"Here, I have just the thing." She leaned over the seat and dug through her bag of paperbacks. "Gayle Wilson writes a great suspense."

"Suspense?" There was a hint of hopefulness in his voice.

"Hey, people fall in love in all kinds of situations. Why not in the middle of some huge intrigue?"

"I guess."

He eyed the cover nervously. Mary suppressed a smile as he opened it and sank back in his seat.

Suddenly, she felt at ease again. She turned and went back to her bag of books. She wanted something funny, something that matched her suddenly buoyant mood. Smiling behind her choice, Mary dove into the Jennifer Drew book that had her laughing out loud moments later.

"So what did you think?" Mary asked hours later when Ethan finally shut the book.

She'd finished her story and had decided that was it for the night. She'd save Cheryl St. John's new one until morning.

"It said there was another one after this in the series. I don't suppose you have it in that bag?" That he'd answered her question with his own hopeful question was enough of an answer for her.

"Just so happens that there are two more to that series and I have both."

Mary leaned over the seat and by the rustling noise Ethan knew she was digging through the bag.

It wasn't the digging that bothered him, it was the leaning. She was leaning in such a way that she emphasized her . . . assets. And emphasized them too well.

Though the author had described a blonde heroine, in Ethan's mind she'd been a brunette. Not only that, she'd looked sort of like Mary — a lot like Mary.

And when the hero finally kissed her, he suddenly bore a striking resemblance to Ethan himself.

The book was entertaining, but reading it with Mary right next to him, with the scent of her filling the cab, with the sound of her soft, sultry chuckles as she read her own book — it was torture.

Torture, pure and simple, and here he was asking for more. What was he, a masochist?

"Here you go." She flipped back onto the front seat, effectively hiding from his view the part of her body that had been driving him nuts. She handed him two books and stretched out her hand, emphasizing another part of her body — a matched set. He was done reading for a while.

"Maybe we should turn out the light and try to get some sleep?" he suggested.

In the cover of night he wouldn't be able to see her and he could try to relax.

Mary shrugged, the movement of her

shoulders emphasizing the perfect purportionality of her body. Ethan fought back a groan — he knew he wouldn't be able to get her out of his mind, no matter how dark it was.

They were getting along, that was all, he thought. Mary Rosenthal was all wrong for him. He was just experiencing some side effect to the powerful, emotional story he'd just read — nothing more.

"Goodnight," she said.

She reached between them to the console and flipped the switch dousing the interior light. "I'm glad you enjoyed the book. Gayle Wilson is a favorite of mine."

"Yeah, it wasn't what I expected."

"You know, that's the problem with so many people. They frequently form opinions about things without ever really looking at what's inside the cover. And because they don't take a look inside, they miss out on something fantastic."

Ethan swallowed hard, wishing he'd never opened this particular cover and caught a glimpse of who Mary Rosenthal really was. She'd loaned him a pillow, but it smelled like her and kept him awake, so he wedged his head between the door and the edge of the seat. He wondered if he could close the book on Mary Rosenthal before it was too late.

As she shifted and her thigh brushed his, Ethan acknowledged the truth of it.

It had been too late from the moment he had opened the pickup's door and crawled into the cab.

DAY EIGHT

"Who's playing again? And who am I rooting for?" Mary asked for the third time.

They'd spent Saturday dutifully visiting with the public and being cordial with each other. They weren't the best of friends, but they were getting along, and things were a lot less strained than a week ago. Whether or not that was a good thing, Ethan couldn't figure out.

He'd finished Gayle Wilson's series and moved on to a series by J. D. Robb. He almost hated taking a break from the books, but today was the big game.

The fly in his ointment was that his tiny television wasn't broadcasting the game very clearly. All he could see were shadows in the midst of a snow storm.

"Who do we like?" He just shook his head in sorrow. That anyone could have grown up in Erie, Pennsylvania and not know which baseball team to root for was just plain wrong. "Cleveland. We like the Cleveland Indians."

He pointed to the hat on his head and the blue jersey with the Indian's head he was wearing. "They're playing New York. We hate the Yankees."

"Why?" She squinted at the screen.

Ethan looked up from the distorted picture. She looked as confused as she sounded. "Because we like Cleveland, so we hate New York." He'd explained it all yesterday, but the message didn't appear to have sunken in.

"Okay," Mary said agreeably. She'd been much too agreeable all morning.

Ethan viewed her nervously. "You're sure you want to learn about baseball?"

"If you can learn about romance, I can learn about first base."

"Point in fact, I knew about romance, just not about the books. And teaching you about first base could be fun, but teaching you about home runs would be more fun."

She slugged him, like a girl who thinks a guy is joking would slug someone. "You know about romance? Tell me the most romantic thing you can think of doing for a girl."

"Wine and candles?"

She laughed.

"Okay, champagne."

As she shook her head, her hair brushed his cheek. Ethan wondered how it would feel to run his fingers through it. He lifted a hand, then just as quickly let it sink back to the television. Liking her was one thing, but *liking* her was another.

"So tell me what you think is romantic." Anything was better than fantasizing about her hair.

Her brows furrowed as she toyed with her glasses. "Romance would be someone thinking of me. Not something cliche, like flowers or candles, but something that would be special just for me. Maybe it would be a song, *our song.* Maybe it would be watching the sunset at the beach. Maybe . . ." She stopped abruptly. "Oh, you get the idea. But we're not talking about romance today, we're talking about baseball. Enough teasing me about the books. You like them well enough."

The only problem was, Ethan was pretty sure he wasn't teasing. Every minute he spent with her, he was becoming more sure he wanted to know more about this lady.

"Damn!" Whether the curse was out of frustration over the tiny television that wasn't tuning in for anything, or concern over Mary who seemed totally oblivious to his growing attraction, he wasn't sure.

"No swearing." Her voice had all the teacher-like primness he'd originally expected. It was only her grin that kept him from believing her act was for real. "Close your eyes."

"I don't think so," he said. "You have a dangerous look in those sky-blue eyes. How do I know you won't take advantage of me when my eyes are closed?"

"Come on, Ethan. I have a surprise for you. Be a sport, just this once. Close your eyes for a few minutes."

Ethan sighed, knowing he'd lost the battle before it had even begun. He closed his eyes and leaned back against the seat. "How long do I have to keep them closed?"

"I'll let you know when you can open them." Her hand covered his eyes and suddenly Ethan didn't mind this little game.

Mary's body was pressed against his, covering his side the same way her hand was covering his eyes. He could smell her. What was the scent that she wore? He wanted to ask, but couldn't bring himself to. He'd find out one of these days and then he'd go order a whole case of it for her.

"Well, don't just sit there in silence, talk to me." His voice sounded strange to his own ear and he hoped she didn't notice. He was suddenly uncomfortably warm.

"About what?"

He'd almost been able to ignore the husky, sensuous quality to her voice, but with his eyes closed and nothing to distract him, he noticed. Boy, did he notice.

He needed to hear her talk, yet dreaded the torture. "Tell me about when you're going to get out of this truck so we can both go home."

Her voice dropped and sounded sad. "I told you, I can't do that. I thought we were finally getting along." Her voice sounded hurt.

Ethan could have kicked himself. He only brought it up because with each passing day the burning desire to get out of the pickup was dissipating, being replaced by another, more urgent desire.

Softly, she continued. "If you want out, you're going to have to be the one to leave the truck, because I can't."

"You've never told me why you're so bound and determined to win this truck." There was something odd going on here, something more than just Mary wanting a new truck, and now Ethan wanted to know what it was.

"I'm not going to now either. Let's just say, I'm going to win, and the sooner you face that, the sooner we'll both be able to get out and enjoy the beach."

"Mary —"

"Okay, you can open your eyes." Her hand dropped.

The first thing he saw was her. Actually, the only thing he saw was her. Something had happened Friday night and whatever it was it was growing stronger. Any thoughts of leaving or winning the truck were totally gone and Ethan wasn't sure he liked the thoughts that replaced them.

"What do you think?" she asked.

He thought he was lost.

"About what?" His throat had suddenly gone dry and his mind had turned to mush.

"About your surprise," Mary said with a low chuckle.

"Huh?"

"Look." She pointed through the window. A television stood against the far wall; a very big television. In fact, it looked just like his television at home.

"A television?" he asked.

"We're having a tailgate party for the big game today. You've been swearing at that tiny screen all week. I decided to avoid the cursing this afternoon." She stuck her head out her open window. "Come out guys."

The pickup bounced as the bed filled with

bodies . . . the bodies of his friends. Barney's grinning face peeked in the back window.

"So, were you surprised?" Barney asked.

"Surprised? I can't believe you guys did this." His life had been full of surprises the last few days.

"Actually, we didn't. It was Mary's idea."

"You?" He turned in disbelief.

Mary grinned. "Well, you were a good sport and tried my books, so I thought I'd give baseball a try. After all, it is the great American pastime and I don't think I'd get a real good idea of the game on that little television you've been watching. So, I asked the guys to bring something bigger and Barney assured me that no one had a bigger one than you, so he broke into your place and stole your television."

Ethan grinned a wicked grin and Mary relaxed. She hadn't been sure he'd appreciate his friends *borrowing* his television, but he obviously didn't mind.

"The biggest, eh?" Ethan asked Barney.

Barney broke in, "Television, Westbrook. No one's got a bigger *television*. If we're talking about other handy appliances, well, Mary my love, I have to assure you that —"

"We weren't talking about anything other than televisions, so you can stop that thought right there," Ethan interrupted.

It took a moment for Mary to realize what was going on. "Oh, Barney, if Ethan doesn't have the biggest . . . ah, appliance, then who does?"

"Well . . ." Barney's grin left no doubt as to whose appliance he was going to proclaim the biggest and best.

Ethan cut him off. "Mary you're a teacher, for Pete's sake. A kindergarten teacher. You can't talk like that."

He was blushing! Big, tough, Ethan Westbrook was blushing. The sight intrigued Mary.

"Teachers are well aware that people come in all sorts of shapes and sizes."

Just to torment him, she added a little more suggestiveness to her voice. "*All* shapes and sizes.

"Enough," Ethan barked, his face aflame and his scowl twisting his mouth.

"How did you get into my place?" he asked Barney in an obvious ploy to change the subject.

"I've still got the key from when I crashed there last year, so there wasn't much breaking. Al loaned us a truck to get the television here."

"Al's using the tailgate theme as a promotional tool. He's having a cookout — hotdogs, chips, and beer all around. And hopefully lots of sales."

Mary allowed Ethan his change of topics, but she wasn't about to forget his embarrassment. Was it the fact that she was a teacher, or just that it was her, that embarrassed him. It was a fascinating thought.

"Your lady's a keeper," Barney proclaimed as he ducked back out of the small window.

"You did this for me?" Ethan couldn't get over it.

Now it was Mary's turn to be embarrassed. She shrugged her shoulders. "Sure. We might be battling over who wins the pickup, but that doesn't mean I don't like you."

"You *like* me?" Laughter edged his voice.

"Well, you've got potential in a macho-male, baseball watching, couch potato sort of way."

"You think I'm macho?" He was eating up her compliments, and turning her words into something she never intended, embarrassing her as surely as she had embarrassed him.

Mary swallowed hard. *Keep it light,* she reminded herself. *Don't think about the Ethan who discussed romance books. Don't think about the way it felt to wake up on his lap, his hands in your hair.*

She pointed to the television. "Isn't something starting there? I didn't think the game was for another half hour."

He glanced at the TV, but his eyes quickly shifted back to Mary. "It's the pre-game show."

"Pre-game?"

"And afterwards we have the post-game show."

"Why do you need shows about a game that hasn't been played or about games that are over?"

She'd never understood people's fascination with professional sports. It was one thing to watch a game where you knew the players, it was another thing to watch men who made millions to strut their stuff.

"The pre-game show is so you can discuss what might happen in the game, and the post-game is so you can discuss what did happen."

"Why not watch the game and you wouldn't need to discuss any of it?" This made sense to Mary, but a furrowed brow indicated it didn't make as much sense to Ethan.

"You just don't get it." He shook his head sadly.

She grinned. "No, I guess I don't."

"Hey, you're not supposed to be talking,"

Barney shouted through the window. "You're missing the show."

"I'll be quiet," Mary promised. "I wouldn't want you guys to miss anything."

She sat back and tried to absorb what was being said, not on the television, but between Ethan and his friends. This Ethan — the one who joked with his buddies, the one who blushed at her teasing — this was someone she'd only met moments ago and she was discovering she enjoyed him a lot.

Too much maybe.

She pretended to pay attention to the pre-game show that eventually turned into the actual game.

Ethan pointed out players and plays, and Mary smiled and nodded at what she hoped were appropriate times during his instruction. And when he finished, she promptly forgot everything he said.

"Come on, come on, come on. Get him!"

"What happened?" Mary asked.

"The pitcher hadn't given up a run the whole inning, but just gave one up to that man there. And see that guy in right field? Well, he caught it, so that's it."

"That's what?" Mary asked, confused.

"Now the Tribe's batting."

"The Tribe?" Mary knew she wasn't stupid, but she'd been watching the game for almost an hour and still didn't get it.

"Our team," he said with a hint of annoyance in his voice.

"I thought we were rooting for the Indians."

Ethan sighed the anguished sigh of a martyr. "The Tribe *is* the Indians. It's a nickname for the team."

"And they're pitching well this game?"

"That they made it through the whole inning without the Yankees scoring is very good."

Mary shut up and tried to follow the game, but her effort was half-hearted at best. She was having more fun watching Ethan than any game. His friends in the back of the truck whooped from time to time and hands flew through the sliding rear window high-fiving and thumping Ethan on the back. Ethan was just as loud, grunting and whooping with the rest of them. This side of Ethan was more than just fascinating, it was cute.

Cute?

Mary smiled and kept the thought to herself. Mary might not know much about men, but she doubted Ethan would like being thought of as cute. She chuckled softly.

"Having fun?" Ethan asked.

Oh yes, she was having fun, but it was

Ethan, not the game, that was the source of her amusement.

He cocked a brow at her. "Are you paying attention?"

"Yes," she answered truthfully. She was paying attention to the man who was sharing her truck. "So explain what's going on now."

"See, I knew you weren't paying attention. This is it, Mare. Cleveland's down by three runs and the bases are loaded. That means if Travis Hafner — he's the guy at bat — can hit the ball, we have a chance, but if he can slam a homerun, we win."

"And the game's over?" she asked, maybe with a bit too much enthusiasm, because Ethan glared at her.

"Unless it's tied, then we go into extra innings."

She sighed. "And we're not done. Guess I'm cheering for a homerun." She attempted to focus on baseball, but her mind wandered to other types of homeruns.

She cut off the mental image that was so much more intriguing than the one on television.

"Mary, he missed."

"A strike?" Her voice was little more than a squeak, and if the warmth she was experi-

93

encing was any indication, her cheeks were flushed.

"Yes." He glanced at her. "Are you okay?"

"Fine." *Strike* probably summed up her chances with Ethan Westbrook. He didn't even like her. Why would he be interested in . . . well, interested?

"Oh come on!" he bellowed.

"What now?" She concentrated on the game, anything to get her mind off Ethan hitting a homerun with her.

"It's a ball!" he shouted. The guys in the back of the pickup let out a collective groan.

"Four of those and he walks, right?" She remembered some of his baseball lectures.

He beamed. "Right. You *are* paying attention."

"I'm a fast learner," she said. But this wasn't the game she was fantasizing about Ethan teaching her.

"Argh, another ball."

"Come on, Travis!" Mary's cheer earned her a smile from Ethan — a smile that sent her heart racing in her chest.

"It's another ball." Mary's attention was riveted on the screen. She reached over and squeezed Ethan's hand. "One more and he walks, right?"

"Right."

"Strike!" someone yelled from the back of

94

the truck.

"And one more of those and it's over, right?" she asked again.

Ethan glared at her, as if it was her fault Hafner missed the ball. "One more strike and the Tribe is done."

"Here's the wind up!" Barney shouted through the window.

"Look at that go," Ethan muttered and then cheered. "Yay!"

"Is it a homerun?" Mary asked.

"It sure is. It sure as hell is!" He leaned over and kissed her square on the lips. The pressure of his lips against hers was quick, but not quick enough to keep Mary from turning breathless.

"Well," she finally said. What she wanted to say was *let's do that again,* but she settled for saying, "Well, alright Travis. I think I like that man."

"Honey, so do I, so do I."

"*Like* him?" Barney yelled through the window. "I don't just like him, I *love* him!" He turned to the others in the back — the whole lot of them were whooping and cheering.

Mary laughed, trying to shake the intriguing sensation of Ethan's lips on hers. He hadn't meant it, it had just been a heat-of-the-moment sort of kiss. "That was great."

"Great?" Ethan sounded insulted. "That was the best game of the season. It was awesome, stupendous, earth-shattering even."

She was thinking more of the kiss than the game. Her mind reeled with the revelation. She'd shared the truck with Ethan for a whole week. The contest had started as just a means to an end, but the more time she was with Ethan the more thinking about the ending didn't hold much appeal — even if it meant she'd own a new pickup.

The truth of the matter was she wanted Ethan. The contest was giving her an opportunity to have him, to be with him, and that fact was an earth-shattering revelation. She wanted to be with him. Winning the brand new pickup and the contest coming to an end didn't hold as much appeal as it once had.

What was happening to her? Logic, normalcy had gone flying out the window with one little touch of his lips.

This kind of passion without thought or reason was something a Sky Blue might let happen, but it was something Mary Rosenthal had spent her life avoiding.

"Twenty questions." Mary was grasping for something, anything, to relieve the boredom.

"What?"

"Let's play twenty questions."

It was Monday night and Al's had closed early. Being stuck in a truck was one thing when they were surrounded by people — staff, customers, WLVH disc jockeys, and sight-seers. But, when the showroom was quiet and just Monroe, the night watchman, roamed the building, the silence could be overwhelming.

Even with Monroe's occasional check-ins to make sure they weren't cheating, it wasn't quite the same as with their daytime chaperones.

"Why?" Ethan asked.

She'd just finished Cheryl St. John's newest book and wished the author wrote faster. Every book she read twisted at her heart and etched the characters there permanently. St. John always left her hungry for more. She needed something to do.

Mary had grown decidedly bored and wanted someone to talk to, but had discovered that Ethan wouldn't know a bid to converse if it bit him in the butt. As if she was talking to one of her kindergartners, she explained, "Twenty questions about each other."

"I don't think so." He shook his head and stuck his nose back into one of J. D. Robb's *Death* books.

"What do you mean, you don't think so? We've been living together a whole week, but I still don't know much about you."

She'd thought they'd been making some headway with the baseball game yesterday, but he'd been quiet ever since; Mary couldn't figure out his silence.

He peeked over the top edge of the book. "Why would you want to? We're rivals."

She'd been asking herself the same thing all day. That he was a rival was getting harder and harder for her to remember, especially since he had kissed her. Okay, so maybe "kiss" was too rich a word.

He'd given her that tiny little peck on the lips. The peck was nothing special, but it could have been. With practice their kisses could turn into something very special.

Forget it, she told herself. Mary couldn't afford to go around kissing Ethan Westbrook. What was she thinking?

She wasn't and that was the problem. "Never mind."

She didn't need to know anything more about him. She knew he was hooked on her books and he liked baseball . . . and that he potentially could give her the kind of kiss she fantasized about.

But kissing him, well that just wouldn't do. She may not have been thinking clearly before, but she was now.

All she needed to know about Ethan was the bad stuff — things that would keep her from falling for the guy. Not that she was planning to fall for him, because she wasn't. He wasn't her type, he was just . . . he was just too close.

It was good that he didn't want to get to know her and didn't want to let her get to know him better. She didn't need to know him better to win the truck away from him — although there was the point about focusing on his flaws so she could stop thinking about how cute he could be. But knowing nothing more about him was probably better. Knowing Ethan, he had no flaws other than his all-consuming passion for baseball. Or he possessed no major flaws that would be horrible enough to make her stop thinking about him obsessively.

She picked up a new book, determined not to think about him anymore.

Period.

End of story.

It was a difficult task, seeing as she was living with this man who had never seemed sexier than at this minute, but she was used to difficult tasks. Creating a normal life in the midst of chaos was difficult, but she'd done it before. She wore normal clothes, had normal friends, even worked at a normal job. If she could do that, she could do anything — even not think about Ethan Westbrook.

"Okay," he said, interrupting her internal reprimand.

"What?" She looked up from the page that she hadn't really been reading.

"I said, okay. Let's play."

She shook her head. "Never mind. I'm reading now."

Ethan inched a little closer. "No you're not. I bet you don't even know who wrote that book. You're just staring at a page, pretending to read while you fume."

"I don't fume." She didn't argue that of course she knew who had written the book because she didn't, and she wouldn't give him the satisfaction of seeing her check.

He laid his paperback down, breaking the binding, but Mary didn't even give him a lecture on how to treat her books.

"I don't fume," she said again.

"Oh, yes you do." He chuckled. "You sit there and quietly seethe over things. You like to pretend you don't care about things, but you do."

"Shut up Ethan." The command was practically a growl. Mary Rosenthal wasn't the type to growl or get annoyed, not even when severely provoked — which she certainly was at the moment.

Ethan didn't seem to notice that she was annoyed. His inability to discern the difference between fuming and annoyance was even more annoying to her.

"Me first, since it was your idea. Why did you become a teacher?" He inched closer.

"Why?" Mary wasn't sure she wanted to play the game, but she found herself thinking about the question. Why did he want to know and how could she explain her reasons to him?

"I like kids."

The explanation sounded lame even to her own ears.

Those three words must have sounded

lame to him as well, because he strummed his fingers on the back of the seat and rolled his eyes. "If this is how we're going to play, we might as well quit now. We have all night and can certainly afford more than three syllable answers."

"Fine." She studied the dash absently, forming her thoughts and feelings into words she hoped he would understand. "Kindergartners are fun. They're so excited about the littlest thing. It's never dull, and I just love seeing the kids' enthusiasm about everything. Teaching is who I am and what I do." After a moment she added, "I think at first I went into elementary education in order to annoy my mother."

"Why would your mother be annoyed?" Ethan stopped strumming his fingers and he focused his hazy gray eyes on her, studying her.

How could she hope to explain Gilda to Ethan when most of the time she didn't understand her mother herself? "My mom used to think that I worried too much about things like money and jobs and security — she still does. She wanted me — wants me — to be more of a free spirit like she is."

"And you're not?"

Mary shook her head and chuckled. "According to Gilda, I have a neurotic need to fit in. I'd argue that she has a neurotic need not to."

"So being a kindergarten teacher means you fit in?"

"Well, I guess I fit in with most people better as a teacher than I would as a Tarot reader."

He raised an eyebrow and the corners of his mouth quirked in a way that suggested he was trying not to grin. "Tarot?"

"Gilda's idea of my perfect job. She reads palms and thought we could go into business together."

This game had been a dumb idea, she decided now that it was too late to stop. She hated talking about herself in most situations, but talking with Ethan on such a personal level was dangerous. It might mean he'd see too much, or she might see too much and that could lead to — a brief image of that one kiss flitted across her mind, shattering her concentration.

"My turn." She tried to focus on questions, not kissing.

"Fine." Ethan was being agreeable again.

Mary watched him, wondering what he was up to. "Why are you a pharmacist?"

"Unlike you, I conformed to my father's wishes. He wanted me to be part of the family business and I never even considered anything else; not since he bought me my first chemistry set when I was five." He leaned back and spread his arms across the back of the seat, brushing the back of her neck.

Shivers climbed Mary's spine and she inched forward, desperately trying to avoid even the most casual contact and the feelings it invoked.

"If you had thought about being something else — if you could be anything you wanted — what would you be?" Her voice sounded shaky to her own ears.

"When I was little I thought about becoming a cowboy, but as it turned out I have terrible hay fever."

His laughter made Mary think the game hadn't been such a bad idea after all. "I can see how that would put a damper on things. So other than being a cowboy, there's nothing else you ever wanted to be?"

He drew his brows together and his mouth formed a thoughtful frown. "I can't think of a single thing I'd rather be. I like what I do. My family drives me nuts and then there's Dad — he doesn't realize he's retired and he feels he has to have his finger in everything, but," he winked at her conspiratorially, "and don't tell him I said this, I don't mind him most of the time."

Mary remembered Charles complaining about missing his time to golf. "It looks like he's learning his lesson. He seems to be having problems with the new computer system."

"Oh, he'll figure the computer system out. Dad just likes to grumble."

They were getting along so well that Mary didn't think it would be wise to remind him of the old adage, "like father, like son." She decided to be safe rather than sorry.

"What other family do you have?" she asked instead.

"I have two cousins, Joe and Pauline — Paul if you want to annoy Aunt Constance, and we all do. They were both working yesterday during the game, or you would have met them. They're not bad. It's their mom, Constance, who's the pain. She thinks the three of us should settle down."

"Are you all that wild?" *Wild.* The word made her think of the fantasies she'd been having about Ethan. If he was half the man she imagined he was, wild was an understatement.

"She doesn't want us to settle down because we're wild, she wants us to settle down and marry. According to Aunt Constance, married life is the only way to attain eternal happiness, though I don't remember my uncle being all that happy when he was alive."

Ah, his aunt was a matchmaker. Gilda was just the opposite; she didn't believe in settling for just one man. According to Gilda, men were a dime a dozen.

"Don't you want to settle down?" she asked.

"I've never found a woman who could hold my interest for more than a few dates, so what are the odds that I'm going to find one who could fascinate me for the rest of my life?"

He was a male version of Gilda. Mary's heart constricted. Not that she wanted a relationship with Ethan. No way. Competing with him for a pickup was one thing, but dating him was out of the question. "I see what you mean."

His eyes narrowed as he drew closer. "There's no man in your life?"

"Not right now." The last man in her life should have been her perfect match. He was a high school biology teacher. He wore tweed. He scheduled their dates a week in advance. He drove a blue Ford Taurus sedan.

He was a total bore.

Mary shook her head for emphasis. "No, no one."

"Are you looking? I could offer Aunt Constance's services." The arm that had been resting on the seat behind her slipped onto her shoulders.

"You'd offer her services not so much to find me a man, but to save yourself." She shifted, hoping it would slip off, but it rested easily.

"And Pauline and Joe," he added with a grin.

"You're such a good cousin."

"I like to think so."

"How did we get here?" Mary was ready to talk about something other than families and dates — anything but dates.

Ethan stretched and the arm was gone. Instead of relief, Mary was surprised to feel a sense of loss.

He shifted, widening the space between them. "I believe you suggested Twenty Questions."

It had been a dumb move. Boredom was better than the unrest she now felt. "Maybe we should leave it at. What was it, two a piece?"

"Something like that. We could pick it up again tomorrow?"

"Two every night?" she asked, even though she didn't know if she really wanted to get to know Ethan better. The intimacy seemed dangerous.

Silently she prayed there wouldn't be many more nights to go. She couldn't afford for there to be. Every hour, every minute with Ethan was pulling her further and further into . . . She wasn't exactly sure what she was being pulled into, and she didn't want to try and figure it out. It was safer to ignore her growing fascination with her pickup-mate.

"Deal." Ethan relaxed against the seat.

"Well, I think I'm going to try and turn in." Sleep was her only respite from her Ethan-centered thoughts and from feelings she wasn't sure she wanted to acknowledge.

Right now she desperately needed the reprieve.

"Would you like to sleep on my lap again?" Wicked hope flickered in Ethan's eyes.

Her heart leapt at the suggestion, but Mary ignored it. He was kidding, harmlessly flirting. He was beginning to see her as a friend. It wasn't his fault she fantasized about more.

"I wouldn't want to put you out." She purposely kept her voice light and teasing.

"Can't blame a guy for trying." He laid his head back against the seat and wedged his head between the seat and the door.

Mary studied him a moment. She was going to miss him when this was over. Though she wasn't as anxious for it to end as she once had been.

No, she wasn't anxious for the contest to end, except when she was longing it would. There was a logic in the thought that Mary understood, but she doubted Ethan would. It was similar to the fact that he could annoy her in one moment, and then inspire fantasies in the next.

She smiled as she thought about trying to explain it to him.

Ethan stirred, changing his position, trying to find a comfortable one. Comfort was becoming increasingly difficult to attain with Mary around. He hoped tonight would be different. Maybe he'd dream about lying in a real bed, maybe about playing ball on Sunday afternoon with the gang. He longed for dreams of freedom, of his real life.

But lately his dreams were full of something else.

Some*one* else.

She was smiling now, a secret little smile. Ethan wondered what she was thinking as she shifted in her seat.

What was it about Mary that bothered him so much? That kiss he'd given her at the game couldn't be the cause.

That kiss had been a quick, heat-of-the-moment kind of thing, not a *heat* of the moment kind of thing. There was nothing sexual about it all.

Just like there was nothing sexual about Mary. She was just Mary.

Sky Blue Mary Rosenthal, trying so hard to conform to her idea of normalcy. Ethan hadn't had the heart to tell her that she was anything but normal. He'd dated enough normal women to know there wasn't anything remotely normal nor ordinary about Mary. The question that haunted him was, why did he care?

DAY TEN

"Day ten," Punch reminded over the phone. "Mary, Mary, Mary, when are you getting out of that truck? You know Ethan's got more stamina, so why not admit defeat now and salvage the rest of your summer?"

Mary generally found Punch's male chauvinism amusing, but today her throat was ticklish, her nose was runny, and she just wasn't in the mood to put up with Punch's nonsense.

"What makes you feel Ethan has more stamina?"

"Honey pie, Ethan's a guy, so of course he has more stamina." Punch's standard comment — guys ruled.

"Excuse Punch, Mary. He gives chauvinists a bad name." Annoyance dripped from Judy's husky voice.

"No problem, Judy. I just consider the source. But, I don't know how you work with him," Mary added.

"Neither do I," Judy muttered.

"Hey, it almost sounds as if the two of you don't like me," Punch cried.

"What gave you your first clue, Sherlock?" Judy asked.

Mary sneezed. "He's a little slow, isn't he?" She could hear the sympathy in her own voice and didn't try to disguise it. Judy Bently deserved all the sympathy she could get, in Mary's opinion at least.

"Bless you," Judy responded automatically. "Slow? That doesn't even begin to describe Punch. *Stationary* might be a better word. He's stuck somewhere in the Victorian age."

"A friend shared her theory about men once," Mary said.

"Do tell," Judy encouraged.

"Oh, yes, do tell," Punch echoed. His voice sounded a bit disgruntled, which delighted Mary.

She smiled at Ethan, who cast her a frown. "Okay, here's where the teacher in me comes out. You're all aware that women have two X chromosomes and men have an X and a Y. Well, what's a Y? An incomplete X, that's what it is. Men don't have a leg to stand on. And because they feel inferior, like our poor Punch, they become chauvinists in the hope of convincing themselves that they're better."

Judy's laughter overrode Punch's roar of outrage.

"Put Ethan on," he said.

"Why, Punch? Don't like being on the receiving end?" Mary chuckled and handed the cell phone to Ethan.

"Yes?" Ethan said.

"Help me out here, partner," Punch said.

"Wish I could, but you've dug the hole a little too deep. Looks like you're on your own." Ethan laughed right along with the women and handed the phone back to Mary.

"Some friend," Punch muttered, then asked a few bland questions until the interview ended.

"And some theory, Rosenthal," he said as soon as he'd signed off.

"My mama didn't raise no fool. Behave yourself Punch O'Brien."

Judy jumped in. "Or else I'm going to call Stella and tell her what really happened last Friday."

"Stel-la-ha?" Mary sneezed the second syllable of the girl's name.

"Bless you again," Judy said. "Stella's the current girl, or at least she was. Punch backed out of a date — said he was sick."

"Was he sick?" Mary asked.

113

Judy snorted. "Heartsick. He met Mitsy."

"Mitsy? My Sunday School teacher had a dog named Mitsy. A yappy little poodle that scared the pants off all of us."

"Well, I thought Stella was scary, until I met Mitsy. I'm sure scaring the pants off old Lover Boy here is pretty high on her agenda."

Mary could hear Punch sputtering in the background, but couldn't make out anything he was saying.

"You two all right over there?" Judy asked.

"Sure." Mary hoped she wasn't lying because right now she was feeling anything but all right.

"We're doing a live feed again on Saturday."

"Oh, good. Punch, sweetheart, you can interview me," Mary promised.

"Okay, you two. Gang-up-on-Punch time is over." He sounded more than a little disgruntled. "We're back on the air in a second."

"Talk to you later." Judy hung up.

Ethan's eyes narrowed. "You enjoyed that."

Mary gave an inelegant sniff. She hoped that the congestion wasn't developing into a full-blown cold. She was under enough strain without getting sick on top of everything. She'd better have Gilda bring her a box of tissues, just to be on the safe side. "Just giving him a taste of his own medicine."

"And enjoying it."

Mary chuckled and admitted, "And enjoying it."

"A little too much. You seem almost at home bantering with the two of them in the mornings."

Mary's throat tickled, but she fought the urge to cough. Maybe she could just will away the beginnings of her cold. "It's not hard. I keep trying to give you a turn."

Ethan shook his head. "No, like Punch said, the phone is a woman's domain."

Mary clutched at her chest in mock horror. "Oh, my goodness, he's corrupted you."

"Honey, I was corrupted long before I ever listened to Punch O'Brien in the morning." He laid the back of his fingers against her forehead. "Are you feeling okay?"

A part of Mary wanted to curl up against him and moan. She wasn't sure if that was the sick part, or the heartsick part — no scratch that, not heartsick, just lust-sick. But whatever part it was, she wasn't giving in to it. "Fine. I'm just fine."

His hand brushed across her forehead as he removed it. He leaned forward a moment and gazed at her. Mary shifted under the scrutiny of those soft gray eyes.

"If you say so," he said after what seemed like an eternity.

She did say so. She didn't get colds even in the middle of twenty sniffling five-year-olds. She certainly wasn't going to get one in the summer, especially not from sitting in a truck with just one man.

No way.

By 1:00 that afternoon, Mary admitted defeat. Ethan had been right, she was sick. Allergies. That was her diagnosis. As a matter of fact she actually smiled when her mother knocked on the door. "Mom?"

"Here you go, honey." Gilda passed a box of tissues and a mug of aromatic tea through the pickup's window. "I brought the tissues — the lotion kind — and some tea. And here, I brought you some extra for later." A thermos followed the mug.

Mary took a sip and sighed. "This one's a great combo, Gilda." Her mother supplemented her palm reading income with a small herbal tea business. She made custom, one-of-a-kind blends for clients.

"Rose hips, comfrey, pineapple weed, echinacea, and a couple other special ingredients. The ragweed count is sky high. I don't think it's a cold as much as your allergies." She reached through the window and felt Mary's head. "No fever, that's a good sign."

"Tea?" Ethan asked, crashing the conversation like an unwanted party-goer.

"Why don't you share a mug with Ethan?" Gilda asked. "You might not have allergies, but all this enforced activity can't be good for the immune system. This will give you a boost."

Ethan took the tea Gilda had poured in the thermos lid and handed it to him. He sniffed it suspiciously.

"Mom used to handle the herb gardens at the commune and she still dabbles with herbal remedies."

"And here, honey. I brought vitamin C, echinacea tablets, and zinc lozenges too, just in case it is a cold." She thrust a small paper bag through the window.

Mary took it in the hand that didn't have the tea in it, giving her mother an appreciative smile. "Have I told you lately that I love you, Mom?"

"You know she's not feeling well when she's this easygoing," Gilda said to Ethan.

"You may be right; I've never seen her like this. Don't you think she'd feel better if she got out of the truck and went home to bed?

Since she's being so biddable, you could tell her to and I'll bet she'd listen." Hope filled his voice.

"Don't hold your breath, big guy," Mary muttered and then punctuated the comment with a sneeze. "Or better yet, do hold your breath — preferably until you turn blue."

She opened the box of tissues and blew her nose, not caring at all how it looked to Ethan.

Before Ethan could come up with a retort there came a rap on his window. He turned in surprise. "Dad."

Ethan's father shoved a pile of papers through the window. "Here, I brought you these. You've got your laptop, so see if you can enter the information on disk, something I can just download onto ours."

"Why didn't you just enter the information as you did them?" Ethan shuffled through the papers.

Charles took a step away from the truck and his back snapped stiff. "Because I was busy with my customers and their needs. I'm not a computer technician."

Ethan tossed the pages in the middle of the seat. "Dad, it's quicker just to put the prescriptions into the customers' files as you go. Actually it's a lot quicker than the way you used to do it."

"No, it's quicker just to bring it to you. It's not like you have anything better to do." Charles moved forward again and leaned in the opening. "How are you doing, Mary? You didn't sound well this morning on the air, though you did give it back to Punch as good as he gave."

Mary smiled. "I'm fine, Mr. Westbrook. Thanks."

"Charles." He flashed Mary a smile that left her no doubt just where Ethan had inherited his charm.

"Charles, then."

"Any plans for leaving the pickup?"

Mary also knew where Ethan had inherited his tenacity from, but she didn't take offense. It was easier to chuckle over Charles' persistence than Ethan's. "No, Mr. Westbrook. Like I keep telling your son, I'm here to win. Why don't you just tell him to get out of the truck like a good boy, and we can all get back to our normal lives? You can golf, I can hit the beach, and Ethan can go back to work."

Charles ignored her question. "Do you want me to send something from the pharmacy down for that cold?"

Mary held up the cup of tea. "No thanks. Mom's got me pretty well fixed."

Charles shifted his position. Mary followed the direction of his gaze. It was centered on Gilda.

"Are you going to introduce me?" Charles asked.

Gilda beamed and leaned into Mary's window, not waiting to be introduced. "Gilda Rosenthal. I'm Sky's mother."

"Sky?" Charles glanced at Mary.

Gilda launched into her favorite subject. "Sky changed her name to Mary years ago, but she'll still always be my Sky Blue little girl."

"Mother," Mary groaned.

"See," Gilda said, grinning, "I frustrate her."

Charles pointed a blunt finger at his son. "I do the same to Ethan here."

"How did our kids get to be such stick in the muds, or would it be sticks in the mud?" Gilda patted Mary's shoulder affectionately.

Charles shrugged. "I don't have a clue. Maybe you'd like to join me for lunch and we can discuss it?"

"Why I'd love to." Gilda leaned forward and gave Mary a quick peck on the cheek. "Drink that tea and I'll see you tomorrow, honey."

"I'll be back tomorrow to pick up the paperwork and the disk." Charles reached through the window and slapped Ethan's shoulder with fatherly affection.

Mary slumped back against her seat as she watched her mother, wearing a hunter green floor-length dress, retreat with Ethan's business suit-clad father. "What do you make of that?"

"I don't have a clue." Ethan echoed his father's words then followed Mary's lead, slumping back as if he'd suddenly become deflated.

"Your dad's not attached to anyone, is he?"

Ethan shook his head. "No. He's been alone a long time."

"Mom had a guy a while back. Dancer, I think his name was. Or maybe it was something like Painter, or Sculptor. I don't know. It was something weird and artsy. Hey, that's it — it was Art. Anyway he's obviously gone. That's why she's been coming over every day."

"Wouldn't it be weird if your mom and my dad . . ." Ethan let the unfinished question remain unfinished.

"Not just weird, it would be scary."

If their parents developed a relationship, then she might have occasion to see Ethan after she left the pickup.

Mary wasn't enthusiastic about the idea.

Either whatever it was she was feeling for him would evaporate when she left the pickup, or it would still be there, just as strong. Neither option was at all attractive to her, so she'd decided that when they left the truck, she wasn't going to see Ethan again. Ending their acquaintance would be easier than pretending she just liked him in a platonic sense. Her fantasies, she was realizing, were definitely not platonic.

But, if her mother and his father . . .

Mary shut off the thought. George had asked Gilda to lunch, not proposed marriage.

Actually, the thought of Gilda having a long-term relationship was so absurd that Mary stopped worrying. Even if the two of them were an item any relationship would probably be over long before Mary got out of the truck.

Ethan thumped the papers on the seat. "Guess I have some work to do."

"Can I help?" she offered.

He stared at her dumbly. "Help?"

"Well, if you tell me what information you need to enter from all the papers, I can read it off while you type. This truck wasn't designed as an office."

She should be kicked for offering to help the competition in any way. She needed distance, well, what little distance she could manage anyway. Cozying up with him and his paperwork wasn't the way to go about it.

"You sure you feel up to it?"

She'd opened her mouth one too many times that morning, so she opted to just nod.

"Well then, that would be nice. Thanks." Ethan pushed the pile of papers toward her and set his tea on the dash. He leaned over the seat for his laptop.

Mary wished they had more room up front to store things, at least Ethan's things. This leaning over, and the view the position presented, did little to strengthen her resolve to keep a safe distance between them. He'd traded his jeans in for shorts, but the shorts did little to disguise what a cute butt he had.

"Well then . . ." Mary drained her tea and cleared her throat, trying to clear her mind of the mental image of Ethan's backside. She never had thoughts like this before she moved into the truck. Just like she'd feared, one strange step led to another.

She set her cup on the floor and picked up the first sheet of paper. "Just tell me where to start, boss."

Ethan typed as Mary read. Her husky voice rose and fell in a pleasant rhythm — so pleasant that Ethan was surprised when she said, "That's it."

"Really?" He was unable to believe they'd finished the entire stack of paper, but the pile on the seat had disappeared and the pile on her lap had grown.

She smiled and pulled her glasses from her face and let them fall on her chest, suspended by that chain she always wore. It made him want to kiss her.

"Ethan?" Mary studied him with obvious concern.

Ethan tore his eyes away from her . . . glasses. "Why do you wear your glasses like that?"

"Like what?" Mary wore an innocent expression and toyed with the glasses absently.

He pointed, and in the tight confines of the pickup almost touched the area the glasses rested against. "On a chain, hanging there."

He dropped his hand to his lap as if he'd burned it.

Mary didn't appear to notice. "I can't

keep track of them. When I'm jumping around the classroom with twenty five-year-olds, it's all I can do to keep track of the kids, much less my glasses. I gave up trying a couple of years ago and bought the chain. Gilda said it makes me look like a spinster, but I'm not worried."

"It doesn't." Ethan's voice sounded choked.

"Doesn't what?" Mary asked. She was staring at him with questions in her naive blue eyes.

Sky blue eyes.

He had to stop thinking about her. He should just let the subject drop, but instead he answered. "Doesn't make you look like a spinster."

Mary inspected him. "Ethan are you feeling okay? That almost sounded like a compliment."

"I — ah," he stuttered.

"Here, why don't you have some of Gilda's tea. You'll feel better. I already do." She lifted the thermos and refilled the lid with the steaming brew.

Ethan took the cup and sipped at the pleasant liquid, but he knew drinking tea wouldn't help. He wasn't sick, didn't have allergies. Tea wasn't going to help. The only thing that would work would be getting out of the pickup and away from whatever spell Mary was weaving around him before he fell any deeper into whatever this was he was falling into.

He might not know what to call it, but he knew what was waiting at the end of the hole he was sinking in — Mary.

"You sure you wouldn't rather be at home in bed?" he asked, more out of habit than out of hope that she'd get out.

She laughed. "Good try, but like I said, Gilda's remedy is working. By tomorrow I'll be my old self again."

He could picture Mary in her bed at home. And he could picture himself next to her.

Ethan took another sip and wished he could say the same. He was beginning to think he would never be himself again.

DAY ELEVEN

Mary didn't have to open her eyes to know where she was. The question was, how had she gotten there?

Oh, she didn't really have to ask how, she knew how she'd gotten there. The actual question she needed to ask was why.

Why was keeping her distance from Ethan Westbrook so difficult? Every night she fought a battle to remain on her own side of the truck, and last night she'd lost again.

Slowly, she moved her head and inched away from Ethan. At least her head wasn't on his lap this time, she'd been merely leaning against his shoulder. The position wasn't quite as embarrassing, but every bit as dangerous.

With her head no longer in contact with his shoulder, but his arm still wrapped around her, Mary reached behind her back and gently lifted his arm.

"Where are you going?" Ethan's voice

shattered the silence that echoed through the showroom.

She jerked away. "Back to my own side. I'm sorry I disturbed you. I don't know why I keep ending up over here."

He inched closer. "Maybe you're less inhibited in your sleep and can act on impulses you ignore when you are awake."

Mary retreated until her back bumped the door. "I don't have impulses."

"Everyone has impulses." Ethan slid a couple inches closer.

Mary was thankful they hadn't traded positions yet. She felt a little safer with the steering wheel protecting her. "Not me. At least I don't have impulses about you."

"Liar. You have impulses. Urges even." His voice was husky.

The sound of his voice sent shivers up Mary's spine.

"Yes," she admitted quietly. "But not about you."

"Not about me?"

"No." It was a lie, and Mary always avoided lying, but this time? This time denying it was for the best.

"If you don't have urges toward me, then why is it you're always looking at me like I'm some sort of treat and you're a kid with her hand in the candy jar?"

"My hand has never been in your jar," Mary protested.

She wasn't counting that one quick kiss or the one night she'd spent with her head in his lap, or last night against his shoulder either.

"Your hand might not have been in my jar, but not because you didn't want it to be. You're like a little kid, afraid of getting caught."

"You're an arrogant, egotistical man." She forgot she was moving away from him and wagged her finger in his face, just as she would if he was a student.

"And you, honey, are most definitely a woman with urges." He caught the finger, raised it to his lips and brushed a soft kiss on the tip before he dropped it.

Mary rubbed her entire hand on her sweats, trying to remove his imprint. "Yeah? How about you? You stare at me all the time. Why is that?"

"Because, I'm a man and you're a woman. We've been here for a week and a half. Of course I'm going to stare."

"Why?" she whispered.

"Because I want you."

He reached for her glasses hanging on their chain and pulled her to him. Mary squirmed, not wanting to move any closer to temptation, but the moment his lips touched hers any thought of escape fled, along with any lingering shreds of reason.

The kiss was soft and slow, lingering sweetly. Mary longed to return it, to give into the pressure that was building in her chest, but she needed to think, needed to analyze what was happening.

Gilda would have jumped right in, but that's not how Mary lived her life. She thought things through before she acted.

With great regret she pushed against his chest.

"Why?" Why would a man like Ethan Westbrook want her?

His gray eyes seemed to glow in the murky light. "Come back over here and I'll show you."

"Show me?"

He opened his arms and it was all Mary could do not to jump right into the inviting flame of passion.

"Admit it. We've been flirting with the idea since the first day."

"I don't flirt," she whispered, frozen like a deer in the headlights of an oncoming car.

"Sure you do, honey. You've been watching me —"

"I have not," she said with a little more strength. Ethan's arms remained open, beckoning her. She should resist. She knew she'd regret it later if she followed her heart in this matter.

"I've been watching you, so I know you've been watching me," he confessed.

"Oh."

He reached for her. "Now, come here."

"Ethan, this isn't a good idea," she said even as she inched toward him. His taste lingered on her lips, tempting her to ask for another sample.

"Then why have we both been entertaining it?" Those all-too-enticing arms caught her and pulled her over the remaining space. "I'll tell you why, because living in this truck is making us both a little crazy." His voice was a whispered caress against her neck.

This was *crazy*. It was the only word to describe why she was even entertaining the idea. Ethan? It would be a mistake, more so than living in a truck.

She wasn't the type to have a casual fling.

Looking at Ethan, the heat of his kiss still on her lips, she realized it wouldn't be all casual — at least not for her.

That was even worse. She could end up with a broken heart if she let herself fall for Ethan Westbrook.

If?

There were no ifs about it. She was about to make the biggest mistake of her life. Participating in the contest was her first mistake, something she'd walked into blindly.

But this?

She was about to walk into this thing with Ethan with both eyes open.

"If we're a little crazy, let's take the jump and go off the deep end. But, eventually we'll get out of the truck and sanity will return." It was a warning, more to remind herself that eventually this would end. Ethan wasn't the cling-to-one-woman type. He'd said as much himself.

It wouldn't do to forget.

But maybe it wouldn't hurt to share one more kiss with him — a kiss she was sure she'd never forget.

She leaned forward and touched her lips to his.

"Mary," Ethan gasped. He'd thought kissing Mary would be sweet and tender, and it was. But with that sweetness came an unexpected hunger. The incongruous mixture was the most exciting thing he'd ever experienced. All the air rushed from his lungs.

He said her name again, though he wasn't

sure why. "Mary."

"Monroe," she whispered in return as a light flashed through the dark showroom.

How could he have forgotten the night watchman? "Just lie still."

"He's coming. I saw his flashlight beam," she whispered, her breath ragged.

A wave of disappointment washed through Ethan. He wanted more, but passion was replaced by a need to soothe her, to protect her. He smoothed her hair and despite her wriggling, held her close. "Just be quiet and be still. He'll just think we're sleeping."

"All tangled up together?"

Ethan laughed. "Honey, he won't care."

"I will. I don't do things like —" She broke off the sentence.

Monroe hummed a flat tune as the flashlight beam played across the showroom.

Ethan relaxed his tensed body and pretended to be asleep. He could feel Mary's body soften as she did the same. From beneath his closed eyes he saw the flash of light as Monroe checked on them. Even after the light and humming faded, they still lay entwined on the seat.

Mary Rosenthal.

Who would have thought that under that prim, middle-of-the-road, suburban attitude there lay a woman who would touch him

133

the way she did?

Ethan knew himself well enough to know that the memory of their kiss wouldn't fade soon. But she deserved more than a teenaged necking session in a parked truck.

Part of him wanted to scoop her up and lead her out of the pickup, take her back to his place and keep her in bed until she forgot all about the damned truck. The other part was afraid — Ethan was honest enough with himself to admit it.

He was afraid to leave the truck, afraid that whatever magic he'd found with Mary would fade when they left their tiny fantasy world.

"Is he gone?" Mary asked.

Ethan smoothed her hair again. Brown, medium length, pony-tailed most of the time. It had seemed ordinary at first, but Ethan realized that seeing her hair wasn't the same as touching it. He stroked the loose strands as he fantasized about Mary leaning over him, her hair curtaining them from the world.

She watched him. In the dim light of the showroom he could see expectation in her smokey blue eyes.

"What was the question?" he asked.

"Is he gone?"

Ethan leaned up and peeked out the

window. "Yes."

Mary pushed against him. "We can't let this happen again. We're competing here and, well, it could get uncomfortable, not to mention potentially embarrassing, if we tried to start a more . . . intimate relationship."

Mary wiggled, trying to escape his embrace.

Ethan held firm, as unwilling to release her as he was to leave the truck. "I don't know about you, but I don't think I can get more comfortable than I am right now." Deciding honesty, or at least partial honesty, was the best course, he added, "Mary, I want you."

She sighed and stopped wiggling, though she held herself rigid. "I want you too, but it won't work. Wanting something — dreaming about it even — is one thing, but reality doesn't always correspond with the dream. When I was little I wanted a puppy more than you can imagine."

"And Gilda wouldn't let you have one?" he asked, content to talk about puppies as long as she was in his arms.

Mary chuckled. "Oh no, you know Gilda, she encouraged me to get one. So we went to the pound and I picked up the most disreputable looking animal anyone had ever seen. I named him Shoop."

"Shoop?"

He felt her shrug, more than saw it in the dim showroom.

"I don't know why. I was only seven and his name was Shoop. Anyway, there I was, the proud owner of a dog, just like I'd been dreaming about."

"But?" he asked, knowing there was a but.

"But I was allergic. I lived with watery eyes, sneezing, and congestion — the whole works — for a week until I could find Shoop another home. Mrs. Allen down the street finally took him. I waved at him every day while we lived in Mumford." She reached out and touched his cheek. "You see, there are some things we want, but can't have."

"Honey, you can have all of me that you want, you won't even need allergy shots first." He added what he hoped was the right amount of teasing to his voice so she wouldn't mistake his intentions.

"I can have all I want physically, right?"

"Just say the word."

Her voice dropped. "What if I told you I want a normal life? If I said I wanted a white picket fence, two point three children, and — I'd say a dog, but that's out — but I'm not allergic to minivans and one would come in handy for the kids."

He sat up, no longer smiling. "If you want a minivan, then why are you here in this pickup with me?"

"I want a minivan some day. Right now I want this pickup." There was a hint of sadness in her voice, as if she knew what his reply would be to her hypothetical question.

"So, unless I promise you white picket fences and vans, you don't want *any*thing?"

Mary studied him, and even in the dimly lit showroom she could see the horror in those compelling gray eyes. "Ethan, like Punch, I have a feeling that you are more suited to the Bitsys of the world than to minivans."

"Mitsy," he corrected.

"The Mitsys of the world. You don't want a relationship, you want to scratch your itch." Mary wasn't about to mention that he was giving her an intense itch as well and though she knew she shouldn't, she was very tempted to let Ethan do some scratching.

As if he was reading her mind, he asked, "Are you telling me that you don't have the itch as well?"

"I'm saying that I've learned that some itches can be cured with calamine rather than scratching."

"So, that's it?" He sounded angry.

Mary didn't want to fight, but maybe fighting was safer than kissing. No maybes about it — an angry Ethan Westbrook was safer than a passionate one. She'd experienced the angry one, but a passionate Ethan was unexplored territory.

"Maybe if we were out in the real world, we'd have a chance, but this situation is just too bizarre. I . . ."

"You want me," he insisted.

"Maybe. But I wanted to spend the summer on the beach too, and right now it doesn't look like I'm getting either thing."

"And when I touch you like this?" He reached over and trailed his hand down her jaw line, down her neck, then stopped, letting it rest gently on her shoulder. "You're telling me you can just ignore that? The slightest touch and you're aching."

Mary might be mixed up about what she wanted regarding Ethan, but there was no confusion about how he made her feel. It was all she could do not to beg him to do it again.

"I don't have to ignore it if you don't do it."

"But sweetheart, the thing is, I want to do it."

Mary sighed. "I don't understand any of this. I live a nice quiet life. I date nice, normal men. Men who are looking for someone to build a life with."

"But you've never built a life with any of them," he pointed out.

A dozen replies flitted through Mary's mind, but instead of using one, she found herself answering with honesty. "I've never built a life with any of them because none of them have ever been able to make me feel like you do."

"And how is that?"

She contemplated a few minutes. "Aching, annoyed, amused. Those are just the *A*s. Shall I go on to the *B*s?" She tried to keep her tone light.

"I didn't hear anything after the aching part." He gave her an almost smile that died as soon as it started. "I want you. Can't that be enough, for now anyway?" He absently stroked her hair.

"I'm sorry, it can't."

She thought he might argue longer, but instead he said, "Is there anything in the Mary-wants-a-white-picket-fence life that says we can't snuggle?"

She eyed him, wondering if this was some new ploy.

"I guess there isn't."

"And you trust me enough to just snuggle?"

"Yes." It was that simple. She trusted him.

He wrapped her in his arms. "Then for now trust me to hold you. Let's try to get a few more hours sleep before the day begins."

He shifted his body and urged her until she was practically lying on top of him, wrapped in his arms. The pickup wasn't big enough for Ethan to totally stretch out, so he bent his legs. Mary had to do very little bending to fit. With Ethan's arms around her, she was more comfortable than she'd been since she'd entered the pickup.

She knew she should be worried about what she had agreed to, but instead she only felt a sense of contentment as she drifted off to sleep with visions of sultry Ethan Westbrook dancing through her head.

DAY THIRTEEN

Judy called at 7:00. "Well, Mary, you're sounding better today. Did Ethan fix you up with something from the pharmacy?"

She wished Ethan had fixed her up. "My mom brought over some herbal tea. I think it was my allergies, not a cold."

"It's been thirteen days. Almost two weeks. How's it really going in that pickup?" Judy asked. "Getting bored yet?"

"Ethan and I are both doing just fine. So many of your listeners have dropped by to say hello that we haven't had time to even think about being bored."

"You two are still claiming there are no sparks between you?" Punch broke in.

She felt the heat rush to her cheeks. "Of course not. We're competitors."

Mary wasn't much of a liar, but she thought she had sounded convincing, even if no matter how many times she thought it, or said it, it didn't convince her of a thing.

141

There were sparks. Just snuggling with Ethan was getting harder and harder. She was having a difficult time remembering why she wouldn't allow it to go further.

Images of minivans seemed very far removed.

Punch sighed dramatically. "Rumor has it that you've had a number of male visitors. Glad you're not going to disappoint them by declaring your undying love for Ethan."

There was a pregnant pause. "As a matter of fact, fellas, since Ethan and Mary obviously haven't been able to kindle any sparks, why don't we see if we can find them someone who will heat things up and tempt them to get out of the pickup?"

"What do you have in mind, Punch?" Judy's voice came right on cue.

Nervousness enveloped Mary in a wave. Whatever the two DJs were up to, it was scripted, and she doubted it would bode well for the contestants.

"Well Judy, I've got an idea. Erie's full of single men and women. Lovehandles, the station where love is more than just a song, wants to prove that love can start in the oddest of places. I talked to the station manager today and we've come up with a way to prove it. We're going to give the person who can convince Mary or Ethan to be the first one out of the pickup a week long Hawaiian vacation on us.

"That's right, the first one out of the pickup, and whoever talks them out, are going on a week long, all expense paid trip to a tropical island. So, Mary and Ethan, there's really going to be no loser. Pick someone you like and just jump out of the pickup and right onto an airplane headed for Hawaii. Sand, the ocean, and margaritas at sunset. Who could ask for more?"

Judy jumped in. "That's right, Erie. The summer is heating up, especially in our brand new Chevy truck. Who's going to be the one to convince one of our resident pickup-ers to get out? Someone's going to show them it's time to call it quits. And, now, let's hear from Big Al."

"That's it," Judy's voice said over the phone. "What do you think about the new twist?"

"I . . ." Mary handed the phone to Ethan. The truck radio hadn't been playing, so all he'd heard was her side of the conversation.

"What's up?" Ethan whispered as he put the receiver to his ear. She watched his smile wilt as he heard about Lovehandle's newest twist.

How did she feel? Men from Erie were going to try to tempt her to leave, but she couldn't leave for them any more than she could leave for Ethan.

Once upon a time, BC — before the contest — Mary might have enjoyed the chance to meet men and look for Mr. Right, but at the moment, she only had eyes for Ethan, even though she doubted he'd remain her Mr. Right after they were out of the pickup. But for right now, he was all hers and it wasn't the potential men who were troubling her — it was the women who were going to try to tempt Ethan who were worrying her more than a little.

Alright, they were worrying her a lot.

She should be happy. Maybe Ethan would get out of the pickup and she'd be free and the owner of a truck with a summer on the beach to look forward to. But somehow Mary couldn't work up any enthusiasm for that prospect.

Ethan's frown said he wasn't any more impressed than she was. He hung up the phone. "Well, this should get interesting."

"You can say that again."

"Why don't you just get out of the pickup, Mary?"

Same refrain. "I can't. Why don't you?" But this time, there was a new verse she wasn't about to reveal: She couldn't get out, and she no longer wanted to.

144

She had no doubt that whatever was growing between her and Ethan would be over when they left the truck. The whole fiasco had started only because of their unusual circumstance. They were living in a fantasy world and she knew their attraction wouldn't survive long in the real world.

"I can't leave either. Dad said we had forty new customers bring us their prescriptions last week. That's not just a little return on my stay here, it's unprecedented."

"So, you're staying strictly for business reasons?" Mary tried to disguise her disappointment.

Ethan reached over and wrapped his arm around her. With his other hand he raised her chin, forcing her gaze to meet his. "Business is certainly a concern, but I have another reason to stay now."

"What?" she asked, needing to hear him say it.

"There's a certain kindergarten teacher who's captured my total attention."

"Oh, has she?" Despite her depressing thoughts, Mary smiled. He could do that to her? Make her forget her worries and forget the real world?

There was a knock on the window.

"Breakfast," said Goodness O'Leary, owner of The Blarney Scone. "Simpson went all out today."

"Oh?" Mary asked, eager to see what was for breakfast.

The redhead grinned. "Homemade cinnamon buns to go with your omelets, and just wait until supper."

"What's for supper?" Ethan passed a plate to Mary.

Mary groaned. "You both know that I'm going to waddle when I leave this pickup, don't you?"

"You were too thin to begin with," said Ness.

"I think you're just perfect." Ethan added, too low for Ness to hear but loud enough to make Mary blush.

"Supper?" Ethan prompted.

The older lady seemed oblivious to the sparks in the truck and continued. "Simpson's making his homemade potato soup. Word passes quick in the neighborhood and we'll be swamped, but I can put aside two bowls for the both of you."

"Please," Ethan said. He dug right into the omelet. "What does he put in this?"

"It's a secret. That man guards his recipes more carefully than he guards his kitchen, which says a lot."

Ness chatted amiably for a few more minutes. "Well, I'd better get back. The first

146

wave of the breakfast crowd was gone when I ran over, but the second wave will be hitting soon. See you all at lunch."

Three hours later Mary's thoughts centered on all the evil things she could do to the WLVH disc jockeys. Lunch couldn't come soon enough. Since early morning, there had been a steady stream of people coming through Al's. The men gravitated to her door, the women to Ethan's. Already five different men had propositioned Mary and there was still an hour to go before Ness came with lunch.

Worse than fending off the men's unwanted suggestions were the umpteen women who wanted Ethan to leave with them. She'd just convinced the fifth man that she wasn't leaving the pickup to pack for Hawaii and had leaned her head against the back of the seat and closed her eyes when someone called her name.

Drat.

"Mary?"

She cracked her right eye. "Barney?"

"Tired?"

Mary's spirits brightened. It was just Barney, not some man who wanted to talk her out of the pickup and onto a plane. "You'd think drowsiness would be the last thing I was suffering from, but just sitting here all

147

day is getting to me. I'm tired most of the time." She stretched and leaned toward the window. "So, what brings you down? Is there another big game?"

He shook his head. "Not this week. We're playing Chicago and they're not much of a challenge."

"Oh, so no tailgate party?" Was that disappointment in her voice? She might not know much about baseball, but she had enjoyed herself.

"I'm hoping there won't be. You see, I'm hoping the contest is over by the game."

Mary's spirits rose. "Did Ethan say he was thinking about getting out?"

She peeked over her shoulder to see if Ethan had heard them, but he was in the middle of some deep conversation with a bubbly brunette.

Fine. If he wanted to flirt with some vapid Hawaiian-vacation wanna-be, that was okay with her. She turned her attention back to Barney, unable to decide if Ethan leaving would be a good thing, or a bad thing.

"No, not Ethan. I was hoping you'd think about getting out. I mean, I . . . we could take those tickets and . . . well, hell Mary, we had a good time at the tailgate party. I'm over twenty-one, have all my shots, and I think we could really hit it off."

148

"Barney . . ." Mary couldn't think of a single thing to say. The other men had been easy to shutdown because she didn't care about them, but she genuinely liked Ethan's friend. He was cute and funny. She didn't doubt that they would have a great time on a trip to Hawaii, except for two things: she needed the pickup, and she was beginning to suspect she needed Ethan just as much.

Maybe even more.

"Never mind, stupid idea." He looked sheepish.

Mary reached out and laid her hand over his. "Barney, I really do need the pickup more than a Hawaiian vacation and, well, there's someone else."

"I should have figured. You're too good a catch not to have been snagged." He tried to smile, but the effort wasn't very convincing.

Mary suspected her own smile was just as strained. "Well, I don't know about that, but if I wasn't involved with someone, you'd be the first person I would call. And I want you to know I wouldn't call just any man. I'm rather old fashioned."

Barney flipped his hand so he could hold hers. "Well, if the guy you're seeing is stupid enough to let you go, you just call me. Hawaii or not. You're a class act, Mary."

"So are you, Barney."

She tried to steer the conversation to safer areas, unwilling to reveal the identity of her 'other man.' Ethan hadn't said anything about them to anyone and she wasn't about to spill their secret either.

Pretty soon she and Barney were laughing, any awkwardness left behind them.

Ethan watched Mary and Barney laughing, holding hands as they visited and he tried to ignore the sick feeling in his gut.

He wasn't the type to get jealous.

He just wondered why Barney hadn't bothered to even say hi. Of course he was up to his windshield in women, but Barney could have said *something*.

He turned back to his current visitor — Patrice, Sherice, whatever her name was — but he just wasn't interested. Unfortunately, he couldn't seem to shake this one.

". . . a strapless tan," she said, winding down from a long soliloquy.

"Uh, that's nice," Ethan managed.

She leaned forward and whispered, "You haven't seen nice yet, but if we go to Hawaii, you sure will."

"Hey," Barney said, finally walking around to his side of the truck. "Just wanted to see how you're doing."

Chartreuse, or whoever, stepped back, still smiling, but annoyance clouded her narrowed eyes. Barney didn't seem to notice her. "So, how's it going?"

"That's what I should be asking you. How's it going at the store? Dad hasn't been by for a few days."

"He's managing the computers and flies out of work every night. We all think it's a woman."

Ethan just laughed. His dad rarely dated any woman more than a handful of times and he'd never felt obliged to hurry because of one. "I won't rule out the possibility, but it's more likely he's keeping a date with his golf clubs."

Barney just shrugged. "Maybe."

"So, what were you and Mary talking about?" Ethan tried to sound casual, but Barney's eyebrow shot up.

"Mary?"

Ethan shifted nervously in the seat. "Well you were over there chatting for a while."

"Just this and that."

Ethan wanted to shake the information out of Barney, but he let it go and went on chatting until Barney glanced at his watch. "Gotta go. Some of us have to work."

"You think this is a picnic?" Ethan asked, with more bite in his voice than he intended.

Barney glanced at Mary and then looked meaningfully back toward Ethan. "I think you've got it made, pal. Just don't mess it up." And with that cryptic message, he walked away, at which point Caprice — that was her name — stepped back up and, with a heave of her ample bustline, renewed her assault. "Now, about that strapless tan. I think you'll enjoy . . ."

Ethan glanced over at Mary and knew that he wouldn't be enjoying anything with anyone else for a long time.

"Long day?" Ness asked sympathetically after she'd chased the one remaining man away from Mary's window.

"Thanks for saving me. And yes, it's the longest day we've had in here so far. Right Ethan?"

Ethan nodded without turning from the woman he was talking to through his window. The good-looking, leggy blond gave Mary a thumbs up while Ethan's head was turned.

So she thought she'd snagged Ethan? Well that was fine with Mary. They'd never claimed to have any hold on each other.

"That bad?" Ness interrupted Mary's melancholy thoughts.

"Not bad at all. Maybe she'll get Ethan

out of the pickup and I can get back to my life," Mary grumbled.

"You wouldn't mind?" Ness asked softly.

"Of course I wouldn't. Why, I'm hoping Lovehandle's new twist ends the contest this week. That will still leave me more than two months at the beach." She was becoming adept at lying.

"And that's all you want?" The look in the older woman's eye indicated Mary's lies weren't convincing.

"That and the pickup."

"If you say so, dear." Ness passed her a bag. "Simpson made you both turkey sandwiches and a salad. There's soda and chips for a snack. I'll be back with the potato soup at about six for dinner. Anything else you want?"

"Not me. Ethan," she called a little louder than she needed to. He turned. "Ness wants to know if there's anything special you want for dinner."

He leaned and looked past Mary. "Thanks Ness, whatever you send will be fine. The Blarney Scone is one of the best parts of this entire contest."

"Well, then I think I'll head back next door to my customers." She gave Mary a sympathetic smile. "Take it easy this afternoon."

"Will do." Mary opened the bag and removed her portion of the lunch. Ethan was back in the driver's seat today, so Mary positioned herself so she could balance the plate on her legs. She popped the tab on her cola and put it in the cup holder.

Though she was tired of living in it, she did love her pickup. In fact, she had always thought of it as *her* pickup, not allowing thoughts of failure to enter her mind.

But now failure was looming in the form of a black spandexed, blond, Hawaiian-vacation wanna-be. And it wasn't the pickup Mary would fail to win. She had every confidence that she could outlast Ethan for the truck. It was Ethan she worried about.

The blonde giggled at something he murmured too soft for Mary to make out. She bit into her sandwich with savage delight.

Men. Who needed them? They were an unreliable, fickle lot. But a new pickup? Well that guaranteed years of reliable transportation.

"I'll come back tomorrow and see if I can change your mind," the blonde said, punctuating the sentence with another giggle.

"Honey, I don't think you can, but you're welcome to try."

Let him flirt. Mary didn't care if he made a fool out of himself if he didn't.

"Something wrong?" Ethan rustled the bag, digging out his lunch.

"Oh Ethan, you big hunk, you. Wouldn't you like to take me to a Hawaiian beach and rub me all over with suntan lotion?" Mary asked in a high giggly voice.

"Oh, so my new friend was the problem?" He grinned. "I thought that might be what was wrong."

"Wrong? What could be wrong about your blond bimbette?" Mary tried to laugh his flirtation off, but she couldn't. Seeing Ethan with another woman, knowing that there would be more just like her trying to snag him bothered her more than she wanted to admit.

"You seem a little upset." Ethan bit into his sandwich.

He was teasing her, Mary was almost positive. "Why would I be upset?"

"Are you going to repeat everything I say?" he asked around his food.

"No." He was exasperating and annoying . . . and occasionally funny and charming. He drove her crazy in more ways than she could count.

"Mary, you're not jealous, are you?" His sly grin said he believed she was and that he enjoyed it.

"Of what?" she asked.

"Of Caprice."

"Caprice?" She started to chuckle. "Her name's Caprice?"

He nodded.

"Isn't that a type of Chevy?" *Caprice?* She probably made it up.

"She's a dancer," Ethan added cheerfully.

"A dancer? Really?"

"Really. It's a private club. She promised to dance for me the entire week in Hawaii, if I'd only get out of the pickup right now. She also promised to let me rub oil all over her body — all over. She wants to work on her tan."

"In a couple years she'll have wrinkles and skin cancer." The thoughts of a wrinkled Caprice, her wonderfully perky breasts hanging to her belly button, and her big blonde hair thin and steel-gray made Mary smile. She'd never thought of herself as vindictive before, but a latent streak had obviously surfaced.

"She claims she's got a strapless tan," Ethan continued.

Ethan watched Mary's wonderfully expressive face reflect every nuanced emotion. Right now her eyes were snapping. She was torn between amusement and annoyance, and he thought the combination was sexy as all get out.

Actually there wasn't much about Mary that he didn't find desirable. He liked the way she looked curled up with a book, the way she wasn't afraid to call him on the carpet. He liked how she fit perfectly in his arms. He liked her determination to go after what she wanted.

He just liked her, although 'like' didn't feel like an adequate description of the myriad of feelings he had for Mary Sky Blue Rosenthal.

"Well, I'm sure you'll find out all about her strapless tan when she's lying on a beach beside you in Hawaii. When did you say you were getting out?" Saccharin sweetness dripped from her voice.

"I didn't. I'm not."

"I thought you and Caprice had it all planned."

"Caprice had it planned. I didn't say I agreed."

There had been a time, not so long ago, that someone with Caprice's obvious qualities would have had him jumping for a chance to rub oil all over her. But that was before the contest.

Before Mary.

The women who'd come to proposition him today hadn't attracted him at all, not even the well-endowed, evenly-tanned Caprice.

"Well, you should go. Think about all the fun you and Caprice could have. And once you're out I can claim my pickup and start my vacation."

"You still want out?" The fun of teasing her suddenly paled.

Mary frowned. "Of course I do."

"And what about us?" he asked.

"Well, you'll be in Hawaii and I'll be on Presque Isle."

"So, when we get out of here, this is over?"

Isn't that what he planned? That once the contest was over, whatever they'd started together was over?

Okay, so maybe it's what he'd planned, but Ethan had begun to suspect his plans had altered. And he realized that he wanted Mary to fight for him. He wanted her to work as hard at keeping what they'd found as she worked to win the truck.

Anger welled in his chest. She was going to have a rude awakening if she thought he was just walking away from . . . well, whatever it was they had.

"What's over? We shared a truck and a few kisses. Whatever we had ends when the contest ends."

"I thought we were building something.

No one said it had to end when the truck doors open."

"But no one ever said it wasn't over," she argued.

"What if I said I didn't want it to end?"

He couldn't believe he asked the question. Ethan was the one who always kept things simple, who tried to avoid getting serious. Maybe the confinement was affecting his mind.

"Ethan, think about it. We have nothing in common."

"You don't think so?" A few days ago he hadn't thought so either, but that had changed. Somewhere along the line the way he viewed her had changed radically.

She shook her head. "I'm a kindergarten teacher and I live a quiet life. Don't get me wrong; I like my life. I planned my life and am happy it worked out the way it did. But I recognize myself for what I am. Quiet and normal. You said it yourself — I'm middle of the road. Not tall, not short, not beautiful, but not ugly enough to send people screaming down the street. I'm not rich, but I'm not poor. I'm just a normal woman with normal aspirations. And I like it that way."

"And what are your goals?" he asked. He didn't simply want to know, he *needed* to know. She mattered, more than he'd thought possible. Mary's dreams mattered.

"A job I love, a home, a family to fill it. I want it all and I don't plan to settle for less."

She'd be settling if she stayed with him. Ethan knew that's what she was thinking, because that's what he was thinking. He'd never dated one woman for more than a couple of weeks. He still hung out with his college buddies on the weekends, watching baseball during the summer, hockey during the colder months. He worked hard and played harder.

And somehow it suddenly seemed so unimportant.

Mary said she'd chosen her life. Ethan didn't think he ever had. Oh, he'd chosen his job, but the rest of it he had just slipped into after college. What had seemed fun then suddenly seemed shallow.

"Middle-of-the-road" Mary Rosenthal. That's how she thought of herself, and maybe that's how Ethan had thought of her at first — but not anymore. He was smart enough to realize there was something different about Mary, something special, something that bore no resemblance to the middle-of-the-road woman she thought of herself as.

Ethan recognized she was special, but

160

wasn't sure what to do about it.

He wasn't sure if he should do anything about it.

DAY FOURTEEN

Caprice was back.

The theme from Jaws played in Ethan's head.

"You've had all night to think about it, sweetheart. When are you getting out of this silly pickup?" She forced breathiness into her voice and pushed her breasts forward, as if trying to emphasize just why he should get out of the pickup and on the plane to Hawaii with her.

"I'm getting out of the pickup seconds *after* Mary here does."

"I can't believe she has anything pressing to do. You could be in here all summer," she whined. "Honolulu is waiting."

"It will have to continue waiting, because I'm not getting out, Caprice."

She thrust her chest out even farther. "You don't know what you're missing."

Ethan couldn't help but notice her body, but rather than entice him, her heaving

162

made him wonder just how strong her bra straps were.

"Maybe I don't know what I'm missing by not getting out, but I do know what I'd be missing if I did."

He glanced at Mary, who was pretending to read, but he suspected was in reality eavesdropping. "I'd be missing a chance to publicize Westbrook Pharmacies, and I'd be missing out on my pickup."

He must have finally driven it into her head, because Caprice turned and stalked away without another word. "I don't think she was impressed."

"You should have taken her up on the offer, because you're not winning the pickup."

Mary was trying to make herself feel disappointed that Ethan had turned Caprice down. If he'd accepted the woman's obvious invitation, Mary would at least have the solace of thinking of him as a rat.

But if he kept this up, she might start to believe he really cared about her. That would be dangerous. She needed to remember he was participating in the contest for the pickup, not for her heart.

Mary didn't want to talk to him, she didn't want to think about him, and she certainly didn't want to have feelings for him. She was going to come out of the contest with a truck and a broken heart.

"Are you still mad?" Ethan asked, moving close — dangerously close.

Mad?

Mary wasn't mad . . . at least not in the angry sense of the word. But if one defined the word mad as synonymous with crazy, then she must be.

Anyone getting involved with Ethan "I'm-just-in-it-for-the-pickup-and-the-publicity" Westbrook had to be more than just a little crazy.

"I'm not mad," she assured him, adopting the angry definition.

He slid closer to her. "Then maybe, just maybe, you're jealous?"

She pushed him back toward his side. "It's broad daylight."

"So?"

"If you recall, Lovehandles invited eligible men and women to come down and try to tempt us out of the pickup. If I'm sitting in your lap, you're going to ruin my chances."

"What chances?" he whispered against her neck.

The feelings that cascaded down her spine and made her heart constrict annoyed her even more. She struggled to break his physical hold on her, even if she couldn't break

164

the emotional hold.

"What chances?" She wiggled in an attempt to move away. "My chances of finding a man who might be interested in a picket fence, van-driving, ordinary kind of life."

Mary didn't add that she suspected she'd never find a man who made her feel the things Ethan did. She didn't say that if he told her he loved her, she'd give up her dream and spend the rest of her life having tailgate parties and watching baseball. She couldn't tell him when she could barely admit it to herself.

He released his hold. "So you're looking at the guys?"

Mary moved a couple inches away. "Of course, just like you were looking at Capped-teeth over there."

"Caprice. And I wasn't looking, but if that's how you feel, maybe I should." His gray eyes narrowed and took on the glint of steel.

"Maybe you should," she agreed, trying to sound as if it didn't matter to her a bit. "After all, we've already decided we're too different to make this into anything long term. You've admitted you're not even thinking long term."

Ethan didn't know what to make of her.

165

One minute Mary was sweet and malleable and the next she behaved like a raving lunatic. He hadn't really flirted with Caprice. He didn't even find her attractive. He'd just been a gentleman, at least until she got too annoying.

What was the matter with Mary?

"Mary?" Calmer now, he turned toward her. He'd never had much experience handling women when they were all worked up like this. His cousin didn't get like this, and although his aunt had a steamroller-type personality, she rarely seemed this upset over nothing. "Honey, I really like you and I thought we were having fun."

"Fun? Just a little frolic to break the monotony of this stupid contest?"

Ethan hadn't heard bitterness like that in Mary's voice before. He knew he'd put it there, and he knew if he said the right words, her pain would ease, but, even though he wanted to, he didn't know if he could take that one irrevocable step. "Well, sure. And you can't deny you had fun too."

"You're right. I can't." If she held herself any straighter, she was going to snap.

He tried soothing her. "Listen, let's just forget Caprice and everyone. Let's just have some more fun until this contest is over."

It was a reasonable plan. Mary was special.

She must know how much he liked her. Of course she did. They were having a great time. He could easily spend the rest of the summer in the truck, as long as she was in it with him.

Mary couldn't take anymore fun like this. She'd already lost her heart, but she wasn't going to lose her pickup as well. "Ethan, we're at a stalemate here. The contest has gone on long enough. You and I know you don't need this pickup, so why don't you call your little friend and go to Hawaii?"

He folded his arms across his chest and glared at her. "No."

Mary used her best teacher voice. "You're being unreasonable. I'm going to win and Barney told me you had season tickets for the Indians. Think of all the games you're missing."

She hadn't thought it was possible, but his glare intensified.

Mary sucked in a deep breath, trying to reign in her rising temper. "Ethan, don't be ridiculous. Who knows what Punch and Judy will come up with next to make this contest worse. Get out."

"I'm not getting out. I'm sitting right here and as soon as all these people leave the showroom, I'm going to take you in my arms and —"

She jerked back, even though he hadn't actually touched her. "You're not touching me again."

Ethan's brows raised in surprise. "Why? I know you're annoyed about Caprice, but you don't have to be. We both know you enjoy it when I hold you . . . when we kiss."

"Shut up."

He had the unmitigated gall to shake his finger at her. "That's not very nice."

"Nice? You want nice?" She was out of control and she knew it.

Mary Rosenthal was lost and the Sky Blue in her was in control. Mary would have sat back and just let things be, but not Sky. Like her mother, Sky was the kind of person to make things happen. "It's time to end this ridiculous situation."

He chuckled. "You're not being reasonable."

"Reasonable? I've dealt with you ever so reasonably for almost two weeks. Reasonable? How's this for reasonable." She leaned over him, her torso flattened against his legs, sending electrical charges coursing through her body. Mary ignored the sensation and pulled on the door-handle, then shoved against the door. "Get out."

She jumped back to her side of the pickup as if touching Ethan had burned her.

He maintained his placid expression. "I'm not getting out."

He leaned over her and opened her door. "I'm not getting out, but you can feel free."

Both doors were open. Their eyes were locked. Mary swore she wouldn't be the first to look away. She held his gaze and ignored the pounding in the center of her chest.

She wasn't going to melt all over Ethan Westbrook again. She was going to get him out of the truck and win it. Then she was going to go back to her calm, normal life.

"Just get out," she said. "You have oceans and women to conquer, and I have a summer vacation to start."

"I don't want any other woman. I l— ."

He reached in her direction, as if he were going to caress her cheek.

Mary didn't want to be caressed; she wanted a truck. She leaned back to escape his touch, forgetting the door was open.

She felt herself falling and reached out for something to hold on to. Ethan reached for her and she grabbed his hand. But it wasn't enough to slow her momentum.

She found herself sitting in a rather inelegant heap on Big Al's showroom floor.

What had she done?

"Mary, what did you do?" Ethan jumped from the cab.

"They're out!" someone in the showroom yelled.

Big Al himself came lumbering to the pickup, followed by the crowd that had gathered in the showroom.

"Who got out first?" he asked.

Ethan offered Mary a hand, but she ignored it and climbed to her rather shaky feet.

Ethan faced Al. "I did. I've had enough of living in a fishbowl. It's time I got back to my life."

"Ethan wasn't the first one out, I was." She stretched her hand forward. "Congratulations, Ethan. I hope you enjoy the truck."

Determined to be a good sport about losing the contest and losing Ethan, she pasted a bright smile on her face.

Losing Ethan. The thought tore at her. She'd known the end was coming, but knowing didn't soften the blow. The contest was over and now they'd both get on with their lives.

She wanted to scream, or maybe she wanted to cry. But she wasn't going to do either, at least not right here, right now. Later she could mourn her loss . . . her losses.

"And who will you be taking to Hawaii?" Al asked.

Smile, she reminded herself. She wasn't sure her shaky attempt convinced anyone, but she kept the goofy grin pasted to her face. "Well, there have been so many wonderful men stopping by. It might take me a couple of days to decide."

"Stay right here. Let me call the radio station and tell them it's over," Al said excitedly. He waddled toward his desk.

"Right, you tell them it's over," Mary echoed.

Salesmen, servicemen from the garage, and customers all crowded around Ethan, sweeping him toward the center of the floor with their congratulations. Quietly, Mary crawled into the pickup one last time and collected her bags.

The Chevy was probably too much for her to handle anyway. She was used to her Pinto. Yes, she'd probably do much better on the bus than in this truck.

It was for the best that the contest was over, she thought.

It was probably for the best that it was over with Ethan too. He could return to work, to baseball games with his buddies, to the variety of women he must have in his life. Maybe even to Caprice if that's what he wanted.

Bags in hand, Mary slipped out of the

dealership. It felt odd to step outside. Everything seemed too big.

She didn't have time to contemplate the feeling. She needed to escape. But she hadn't thought ahead. She wasn't sure what to do now that she was out.

She spotted the restaurant that had fed them. That's it, she'd go to The Blarney Scone and call a cab.

Oh, she could call Gilda, but Mary didn't think she was up to the interrogation her mother would put her through. She wanted to forget this whole thing — the pickup, Ethan, and the feelings she didn't want to admit, even to herself.

She entered the restaurant for the first time. Old fashioned booths lined the walls and a generous counter bordered the waitress station. Mary dropped her bags to the left of the door where rows of hooks lined the wall.

She scanned the room, searching for Ness, but she hadn't needed to bother.

The large redhead lumbered over to Mary. "So it's over?"

"It's over." Mary wasn't talking about the truck, though Ness didn't know that. The thought sliced at Mary. "Do you have a phone I can use to call a cab? I seem to be without a ride."

"He won?" Ness asked.

"I lost." She should be upset about losing the pickup; she truly needed the transportation. But she couldn't work up even one sincere regret about it.

She'd lost Ethan. That was the thought that was tearing her apart.

Yet she'd never actually *had* Ethan. She'd just sort of borrowed him, and now she had to give him back. That hurt even more.

"Wait here," Ness said. She walked through a swinging door that Mary assumed led to a kitchen and cracked it. "I'm leaving," she bellowed.

A short, balding man pushed through the door. "Where are you going?" His voice boomed in a way that more than made up for his slight stature.

"I'm taking Mary here home."

"Mary?" His gazed at Mary, giving her a thorough once over.

"From the contest. She lost."

She'd lost. Mary knew it in her head, but her heart kept whispering, "Maybe not." How stupid could she get? It was over.

"Really, Ness, you don't have to —"

"I don't have to do anything but pay taxes and die. One I resent and the other I'm not quite ready for."

"Or you could say that the powers that be

aren't quite ready for you," the man countered. He stuck his hand out toward Mary. "Simpson. Simpson Sutton."

"Pleased to meet you, Simpson. I'm glad I have an opportunity to thank you for all the delicious meals. When I look back at this contest your meals are going to reign in my memory as the highlight."

What a nice, normal thing to say, she thought. Sky Blue Rosenthal was dead, and middle-of-the-road Mary Rosenthal was back. Mary paused, mourning the loss of her alter-ego.

"You go take this poor girl home," Simpson said to Ness. "She probably wants a good bath and then a stretch-out on a real live bed. And when you start missing my cooking, you stop by and I'll make you whatever you like."

"Your potato soup, maybe?"

He beamed. "A woman of taste," he said to Ness.

"Now you've done it." Ness led Mary toward her bags at the door. "His head was swollen enough. Now it won't even fit through the door."

"She loves this big bald head." Simpson marched back into the kitchen.

Ness chuckled and picked up the biggest bag. "Goodness help me, but I do."

Mary picked up the smaller remaining bags and followed Ness, eager to return home.

"You and Simpson?" she whispered.

Ness didn't answer until the two of them were ensconced in an old blue delivery van. "Simpson and me. I still can't get over it. We've worked together for years, but it wasn't until recently that I found out he cared."

Mary empathized with the feeling. "So you never knew?"

"And I might never have known, but my conniving niece made sure we couldn't ignore our feelings for one another. We're getting married in a couple months. Tuxes, reception, the whole works. My niece even convinced me to get a white dress and a veil. Can you see me dressed all in white? Someone is likely to mistake me for a cloud and pull out their umbrella. Where to?"

Mary snapped her seatbelt. "I'm at Thirty-third and Old French. And I'm sure you'll look lovely." It wasn't a lie. Goodness O'Leary might not be beautiful by conventional standards, but she was truly beautiful beneath her gruff personality.

Ness drove as though she was in a Grand Prix race. "For what Maize paid for my dress, I'd better look at least presentable."

"I'm sure Simpson realizes what a lucky man he is." Mary gripped the dash and prayed she would be lucky enough to make it home in one piece. Her heart might be broken, but she didn't need the rest of her body to follow suit.

"That old fart?" She chuckled as she bolted past a yellow light. "Probably wouldn't recognize his luck if it bit him in the butt. What about Ethan?"

"What about Ethan?" Mary exhaled the breath she'd been holding. "He knows how lucky he is. He's driving home a new pickup after all."

"And you?" Ness pressed.

"I lost. What more is there to say?"

"Does he know how lucky he is to have you love him?"

Mary forgot all about the fact that she was probably not going survive the car ride.

"He doesn't know," she whispered.

"And you're not going to tell him, are you?" Ness shook her head. "You two are as dense as Simpson and I were all those years. You should tell him how you feel."

Mary shook her head. "We want different things. We don't fit."

"Didn't you fit right in with his friends when you planned that tailgate party?"

"That's different. I had to be there."

"You didn't enjoy yourself?"

Mary thought about how caught up she'd been in the excitement of the game.

"Yes, I enjoyed myself," she admitted.

"Well, you'll do what you want and far be it from me to meddle. You should think about what you want and what you're willing to risk to get it." She slowed the car as they reached Mary's intersection. "Which one?"

Mary pointed.

Ness stopped in front of the house. "And no matter what you do, you come in and visit Simpson and me sometimes. I'll send you an invitation to the wedding."

"Deal." Mary leaned over and hugged the woman. "Thanks for everything."

"Just go in, unwind and think."

Mary nodded, but as she trudged up her walk she knew her silent agreement had been a lie. She wasn't going to think about the pickup she'd almost won, or about the man she'd loved for such a short time.

DAY FOURTEEN — LOSER

Simpson was right; she needed a long, hot bath and then a nap in a bed . . . a real, stretch-out-to-sleep sort of bed.

She didn't allow herself to check her answering machine. She was sure Ethan wouldn't have called and she wasn't interested in talking to anyone else.

Tomorrow she'd do the interview for Lovehandles and clear up any other loose ends. Then she'd head to the beach . . . on a bus.

Somehow the thought of taking the bus didn't seem nearly as unpleasant as she thought it would. Just like the beach didn't sound nearly as wonderful as she thought it would.

Without Ethan, everything seemed sort of flat and gray. Somewhere along the line, winning the truck had lost its urgency. Because of Ethan.

Everything had changed because of Ethan.

She was going to have to get over him. He was certainly over her already. Maybe when he drove the Chevy, he'd occasionally spare a thought for the funny little teacher he'd spent a couple weeks with.

She shook her head and realized she was standing in her doorway.

She needed to do something . . . something normal.

A bath.

That was where she'd start.

She left her bags where they were and walked down a hallway into her small bathroom. Somehow things seemed different.

She turned the faucet and started her bath. Yes, this was just what she needed. The phone rang, but Mary ignored it. Padding into her room she pulled clean clothes out of her closet — clothes she hadn't worn in two weeks — and wandered back into the bathroom.

A knock sounded on the door. She'd ignore it, just like she'd ignored the phone. There was no car in the drive. Whoever was out there wouldn't know she was home. The visitor couldn't tell, and Mary wasn't about to let him or her know.

The bell rang, accompanied by insistent knocking.

She wasn't going to let anyone in, but it couldn't hurt to peek out. Not that she expected it to be Ethan. No, she didn't expect to ever see him again unless she was getting a prescription filled at Westbrook Pharmacy, which was something she would never do.

Mary peeked out the front window. Tears filled her eyes, but she brushed them aside. No matter what she told herself, she had hoped it was Ethan. She should have known better.

Gilda stood on the porch wearing a fluorescent pink top over tight spandex pants.

"Sky Blue, I know you're in there and I'm not leaving until you open up," Gilda shouted.

The neighbors were going to have a conniption. Knowing full well that Gilda would follow through on her threats, Mary undid the locks and opened the door. "Mother?"

Gilda waltzed into the house and headed into the living room. "So you lost and now you're going to sink right back into the life you'd left behind."

Mary followed. It seemed all her life she'd been following some set of rules she'd mapped out — rules that had always seemed smart.

Now they felt confining.

"I haven't left anything. I liked my life and I still do. I took a small detour, but now I'm back on track."

More than anything, she wanted to go back — back to the truck, back to Ethan. The life that had always seemed so safe suddenly seemed claustrophobic.

Gilda sat on the couch and patted the cushion next to her. "You can't lie to me. You wanted the pickup, but you wanted the man more."

"Mother." Gilda might not be the most normal mother in any conventional sense of the word, but like all mothers, she thought she knew what was best for Mary.

"So now you have no pickup, no money for a new car, and no Ethan. The question is, which loss bothers you more?"

Mary sat next to her mother. "The pickup would have been nice, but there are buses. And I never really had Ethan to begin with. I've lived without a man all these years, so living without Ethan now won't be tough."

Her heart constricted, recognizing the words for what they were — lies. All lies. But she wasn't about to admit that to Gilda.

"And the trip to Hawaii?" Gilda asked.

"I don't want it."

Mary couldn't face going.

She'd thought about asking Barney, and

stressing that they could make the trip as friends, but she just couldn't work up any enthusiasm for it. The trip would remind her of the contest, which would remind her of Ethan. Presque Isle would still be there if she decided she wanted a beach.

"Well, I do."

Mary's head jerked up. "Mother, I don't want to go to Hawaii with you." Barney would be a better choice. At least he wouldn't nag.

"Although I love you, I don't want to go with you." Gilda laughed. "I've got a date to take."

Mary almost sighed with relief. When there was a man around to distract her, Gilda tended to give Mary more breathing room. "A new man?"

"This one's a lot different than the others." Gilda wore a funny look.

If it were anyone else, Mary might say she appeared lovesick, but Gilda didn't fall in love. She liked men, frequently had one in her life, but she didn't make commitments and she didn't talk of love, not ever. She was too much of a free spirit.

"Different how?"

"Different in that I think I love him."

If Gilda had told her that she planned on becoming a nun Mary wouldn't have been

182

more shocked. "What?"

Mary couldn't think of anything else to say. "Who? When?"

Smiling in a secretive way that made Mary nervous, Gilda said, "Well, you'll never guess, so I won't make you try. It's Chuck."

"Chuck?" Mary searched her mind for her mother's friends and couldn't remember a single Chuck among them. "Doesn't ring a bell."

"Westbrook," Gilda added.

Mary choked. "Charles? Charles Westbrook? Ethan's father. *That* Charles?"

"The one and only, and it appears the one and only for me as well."

Her mother had never before talked of love. Mary felt overwhelmed. She was experiencing too many emotions about the contest and about Ethan to sort them out anymore.

She needed to cry. She needed to throw something. She needed Ethan. The thought snuck in and chased all the rest away.

Her mother, she would concentrate on Gilda. "But how, when?"

"Remember that day I met him at the pickup and we went out to lunch?"

Mary nodded slowly, as if she was afraid too much nodding would start the room spinning.

183

"We went out to lunch and didn't leave each other until the next day at breakfast. Now that Ethan's out of the pickup, Chuck doesn't have to work anymore. I want to take him on the trip to celebrate. I love him. It's fast and unexpected, but there it is. I love him."

Her mother was in love? Being in love, in a monogamous relationship, was a hundred and eighty degree turn around. Next thing she knew her mother would be cooking Sunday dinners and inviting the family over.

"The tickets are yours," Mary said weakly. She would have groaned if her mother hadn't looked so radiant. She would be connected to Ethan through her mother if this thing with Charles — she couldn't think of him as Chuck — lasted.

Mary's heart plummeted. She was possibly going to have to spend time with Ethan on holidays and at family gatherings. She would have to pretend nothing had happened, that he hadn't filled up a hole in her heart she didn't even know she had.

"I want to pay you for the tickets," her mother said.

Mary shook her head. "I wouldn't think if it."

"But I would." She reached into one of the robe's pockets and pulled out a check.

"Here's three thousand dollars. It should get you some kind of car. Of course not anything as nice as the Chevy truck, but something that will get you around town."

Mary didn't know what to say. Her world was turning topsy-turvy. Too confused to mount a convincing argument, she simply leaned over and hugged her mother. "Thank you. I'll pick up the tickets at the radio station tomorrow. Is that okay?"

"Fine." Gilda grasped Mary's hand and studied the palm. "I'd ask if you were going to be okay, but I can see for myself that you will."

"What do you see?" Mary asked, despite herself.

Gilda traced a line. "That your life is about to be turned upside down."

Mary had just had the same thought. She jerked her hand away and rubbed it against her navy sweats. It was unnerving when her mother hit a psychic nail on the head. "My life was turned upside down, now I'm turning it upside right again."

"If you say so, dear." Gilda rose and started toward the door. "I'll see you tomorrow afternoon, okay?"

Mary trailed behind her. "Fine."

Gilda opened the door and turned. "Mary, my love, you've spent so many years trying

185

to prove you were my opposite. I know I baffle you as much as you baffle me."

Mary couldn't deny that she didn't understand her mother's lifestyle.

"I love you," she said instead of arguing.

Gilda hugged her. "I love you, too. Love you enough to be honest with you. I know you've worked so hard at being different from me, worked so hard at fitting into a nice little square slot. But honey, I have to tell you that everyone has a bit of a circle in them. You might have created yourself, chosen your path, but on that 'Mary road' you've chosen there's still a touch of Sky Blue. And Sky wouldn't let the best thing that's ever happened to her disappear."

Gilda's gaze held hers for an uncomfortable moment, until Mary averted her eyes. "I don't know what you mean."

Gilda hugged her again. "Yes you do, but I won't push. Just think what your life will be like without Ethan in it."

"I never said I wanted Ethan in my life."

"No, I did. And I'm telling you that sometimes you've got to take a chance. Life can't always be orderly and safe. Sometimes you've got to take risks in order to find the path you need to be on." Gilda smoothed Mary's hair. "Think about it."

Mary finally noticed the vehicle sitting in

her driveway. A VW van. "You bought it?"

"I told you, it reminded me of the van you were conceived in. You know, he wanted to marry me, your father."

Gilda had never refused to talk about Mary's father, but she'd never instigated conversations about him either.

"You never told me that before," Mary said softly.

"He did, but I didn't think I was ready. By the time I decided I was, he was gone."

"I don't have that fear of commitment. Ethan does."

"If your dad had been a bit more patient with me, things might have been different. But he had his dreams, just like I had mine, and neither of us were willing to compromise."

Mary was growing more and more confused. "You're telling me to compromise? Why *me?* Why not *him?*"

"I'm telling you that if you love him, really love him, then you should be willing to let him move at his own pace. You've only known the man two weeks."

"I wasn't talking engagement rings."

Gilda chuckled. "Go find Ethan and tell him you want a boy-toy and that you've decided he would fit the bill. Have fun. Live a little. You can't neatly plan every aspect of

187

your life."

"Good-bye, Mother."

Gilda's eyes widened in an innocent expression. "I know I've annoyed you when you call me mother. I'm getting out of here before I get in more trouble."

Mary closed the door and retreated to her bath. It had cooled considerably, so she added more hot water and sank into the fragrant bubbles. She tried not to think about Ethan or Gilda, but she couldn't seem to help herself. What did Gilda want her to do? Throw herself at the man?

They hadn't really had a relationship. They'd never spoken of the future. He had the truck he wanted and Mary had . . . well, Mary had the life she'd planned.

A nice, quiet, safe and absolutely normal life.

That should be enough.

It should be.

Her life was neat and simple. She knew what to expect and she liked it that way. It was like the bath, smooth placid water. But she hadn't spent her time in the pickup longing for a bath. She'd been longing for the beach with its wild unpredictable waves.

Her life was a bath. Maybe what she'd secretly been longing for was a beach. Maybe what her life needed was Ethan.

Things with him would never be boring, predictable, or placid.

Mary noticed the bath water had cooled yet again. This time she didn't rewarm it. She rose and reached for a towel while at the same time she reached a conclusion. A tepid life wasn't enough — she wanted Ethan.

She wanted fire and passion.

She wanted to take a chance. Maybe she'd end up being hurt. Maybe he'd decide the Caprices of the world were more interesting after all. But she'd never know if she didn't try.

For once in her middle-of-the-road life she was going to listen to Gilda and do something dangerous and crazy.

Two hours later she parked the tiny blue Cavalier that Al had offered to let her try out for the day. It seemed to work and it was in her price range. If she overlooked the rust and the dents, Al assured her that it was a solid car. If she took it as is and saved his garage all the body work, he would be letting it go for a steal.

Mary was probably going to take the car and get on with her vacation, but first things first. She still couldn't quite believe what she was about to do. If she fell on her face, she'd blame her momentary insanity on her mother.

She sat in the car staring at the pharmacy. It was the original store, the one from which Ethan ran the small chain. Gilda had let it slip that he closed the store tonight and that he generally stayed an hour or so after closing finishing up the day's paper work.

He'd be in the dark building all by himself right now.

He wouldn't be expecting Mary, not after their fight — the fight she had started.

Should she or shouldn't she?

She gripped the car door's handle, but she didn't pull. She couldn't quite work up to it just yet.

What if he didn't want her, not even for a casual relationship?

Then she'd be no worse off than she was right now, she convinced herself.

She forced herself to get out of the car, walk to the door of the pharmacy, and peer into the dim interior. No Ethan.

Maybe he'd left early? Or maybe he was celebrating his freedom? Maybe with Caprice?

She missed Ethan already, darn his hide.

Getting back in the car, she dropped her forehead against the steering wheel and groaned. All she wanted was to find Ethan.

190

One way or another she was going to do just that. Gilda would say she just needed to positively align the universe in the direction she wanted it to go.

The direction she wanted to go was toward Ethan. She concentrated on him and turned the key in the ignition one more time. The car purred.

Now to find Ethan.

DAY FOURTEEN — WINNER

Ethan couldn't contain his impatience much longer.

Where was she? He'd paced her porch for three hours.

Was she out with one of the men that had flocked to her side of the pickup? Mary might not be showy like the Caprice's of the world, but far too many men had now had the opportunity to discover just how beautiful she was. What if she was with one of them right now, planning that trip to Hawaii?

At the thought his hands clenched at his side as he waited.

Waiting. That's all he'd been doing. He wanted to do something. The burning in his gut demanded action, but there was nothing he could do but wait.

I I—

He'd wanted to tell her *I love you.* He wanted to say the words he'd never said

192

before. And now he knew why he'd never said them to a woman. He'd been waiting for Mary. Not just some woman.

The woman.

The only woman who would ever suit him.

Maybe she'd used those tickets to Hawaii. Who would she have taken? Not her mother.

Which guy? The one with the ponytail? No, he looked all artsy and that was more Gilda's kind of man than Mary's.

No, Mary would probably choose the tanned blond in the three-piece suit. Yeah, he had looked like a marry-me kind of guy. Mary was probably out with him now, picking out china patterns or whatever engaged women did.

Well, she could just unpick the china *and* the man. She wasn't marrying any three-piece suit. She'd be bored to death in a matter of weeks. She liked to think she was so different from her mother, that she was quiet and unassuming, but he'd learned the truth. Mary was a passionate woman, and she needed someone to remind her of that fact.

She needed Ethan; he loved her.

Where could she be?

As if on cue, a blue Cavalier pulled in the driveway and Mary Sky Blue Rosenthal got out.

"You're here," was all she said.

He couldn't tell if she was pleased to see him or not. Either way, Ethan drank in the sight of her as she walked up onto the porch. He had her now, and she might not realize it, but there was no way he was letting her go again.

"We need to talk," she said, reaching beyond him and putting a key into the lock.

"You're right, we do, but first I need something else. Let's go inside, Mary."

She unlocked the door, but didn't open it. "What do you need?"

"I need you. I missed you. Every minute we were apart, I missed you." Ethan was the one who opened the door and let himself into her house.

It looked warm and inviting. Full of red hues and comfortable looking furniture. And books. Shelves stuffed with books.

It looked like a home.

It looked like Mary.

"I missed you too," she told him, following him into the house and shutting the door behind them.

The admission calmed some of the fury beating through his blood stream.

"That's it? You missed me?"

"Yes." She nodded slowly, eying him cautiously. "It didn't take me long before I realized I made a mistake."

"You're right, you did. You left me."

"I shouldn't have lost my temper. I never do, or never did until now. It was a mistake. Leaving like that. I loved . . . being with you."

For a moment he'd thought she was going to say she loved him.

He hadn't realized how much he wanted to hear her say those words until she didn't.

"Where have you been?" he asked.

"Looking for you. I wanted to talk to you. The way things ended . . ." She shook her head, unsure what to say now that they were together.

"Sounds serious," he said, reaching out and brushing an imaginary piece of hair from her face just so he could touch her, make the slightest contact with her.

"It is. I . . ." She let the sentence fade as she worked at putting her turbulent emotions in a coherent form.

"If you want to wait, you can tell me later," Ethan offered gently. "You see, I have something I want to say."

He took a deep breath and said the words. "Mary, I love —"

At the same moment Mary blurted out, "Ethan, I love you."

They stared at each other a minute and

slowly it felt as if a vise loosened and Ethan's heart could beat again.

"I —" he started, but Mary held a finger over his lips.

"Sh. I need to say this all at once or it will never get said."

She took a big breath and decided to get it over with all at once. "I love you and my rational Mary-side knows it's too soon. She knows that two weeks in a Chevy truck isn't enough time. But Sky Blue knew the first day that we were meant for each other. She'd probably offer to pull out some tarot cards or read your palm and try and prove it to you, but Mary won't let her."

She smiled. "I know it sounds nuts, but there it is. I love you. And I know you said you weren't looking for the American dream. You don't want a house, a family, or a white picket fence."

"And a minivan," he added.

Mary knew that letting dreams die should hurt, but losing Ethan would hurt more. There was barely a twinge of regret as she said, "Or a minivan. I know you think those things are what I want, and maybe I did, but then I met you."

She raised her eyes to his. "Ethan, I've realized that the only thing I want is you."

"Done?" he asked. "It's my turn?"

Mary simply nodded. Her breathless confession had left her empty. She held her breath and waited.

He thrust his hand in a pocket and handed her the small object he extracted. "Here."

He wore an enigmatic smile, confusing her all the more.

Afraid to hope that he felt the same way about her, she opened the velvet box with trembling hands. A key tumbled into her palm. Puzzled, she glanced up.

"Ethan?"

"I promised the truck to Dad. I considered buying you an engagement ring and giving it to you when I asked you to marry me, but I wasn't sure what to get. The Mary part of you would want something traditional, but the Sky Blue part, well, I was thinking of trying to find something as blue as your — her — eyes. I just don't know if I can find the perfect stone though, so I thought we'd search together."

"Marry?" Confused, she held the key out, unable to decipher what Ethan was saying. "Date."

"Marry," he assured her. "The key's to a minivan. You said you wanted one. I picked out a great maroon Chevy Lumina. If you want something different, Al said we could trade it in."

"A van?" Mary's mind felt as thick as chocolate pudding. Ethan pulled her into his arms and she went in a state of numbness. She needed to touch him while she tried to sort out what was happening.

Ethan seemed to sense her need and held her close. "When I found myself loving you, I discovered that white picket fences and minivans were looking more appealing than I'd ever imagined they could."

"Loving me?"

She could feel his chuckle rumbling reassuringly in his chest. She snuggled even closer, listening to the words echo there.

"I tried to say so this afternoon. Honey, you're a teacher, but right now you're a little slow on the uptake. Love you. I love you, Mary Sky Blue Rosenthal." His voice dropped. "And, the van has built-in child restraint seats."

"Ethan?"

"It's a little odd, I guess, for a proposal, but then nothing about this relationship has been normal. I think maybe normal is a highly overrated virtue. Plus, I think some of your romance authors would be proud of us."

He paused and Mary knew she should say something, but she couldn't seem to figure out what.

Gilda had said her life was going to turn upside down and that's how she felt — upside down and inside out. And hopelessly, helplessly in love.

"Are you going to answer me, or leave me here babbling all night?"

The prompting was all she needed. She twisted and wrapped her arms around his neck. "Yes."

There were no remnants of her old doubts and fears. Wrapped in his arms she knew just where she belonged.

EPILOGUE

"It's two o'clock on the nose here at WLVH Lovehandles, where love is more than just a song. This is Punch O'Brien."

"And Judy Bently. Saturdays aren't our normal spot, but today is special. We're here to bring you our first live wedding broadcast."

"Weddings —" There was more than a tinge of disgust in Punch's voice.

"Not today, Punch," Judy scolded, interrupting his imminent diatribe.

He snorted and continued. "For those of you who weren't around this summer, you missed a real scorcher. Ethan and Mary spent two weeks living in a brand new Chevy truck, part of a contest sponsored by Lovehandles and Big Al's Autos."

"Ethan won the truck. But later we found out he won more than just that — he won the heart of our Mary as well." Judy's voice dropped to a whisper. "And the organ is

200

starting to play the processional. Here comes Mary in a traditional white dress, looking like Cinderella come to life." She sighed.

"Seems our Judy has a romantic streak. All I see when I look at Mary is the end of Ethan's carefree existence."

"I mean it — not today, Punch," Judy insisted. "Mary's reached Ethan and she's taken his hand. The minister is talking. What a day for WLVH. We've always said Love-handles was where love was more than just a song, but now we've proven it."

"Sentimental hogwash," Punch muttered.

Judy ignored him. "They're reciting their vows," she whispered. Judy took a deep breath. "The minster is announcing Mr. and Mrs. Ethan Westbrook to the guests and the two of them are walking back down the aisle together. I wish all of you could see how happy they look."

"Let's wait and see them in five years when they have a huge mortgage payment and a couple snotty-nosed kids. Romance tends to fade and all that's left is two frazzled strangers who stay together for the sake of the kids. We'll see how happy — umph!"

Mary stood on the church's front steps and

watched Ethan run around the side of the building. Puzzled, she turned to her mother. "Where's he going?"

With a knowing smile, Gilda took Mary's arm. "Watch."

Moments later, cans tied to the bumper, the Westbrook Pharmacy logo emblazoned on the door of *the truck* — driven by a smiling Ethan — pulled around the corner.

"Hey babe, looking for a ride?" He leaned over and opened the passenger door. "Climb in."

Charles appeared at her side and offered her a hand. Impulsively, Mary kissed his cheek. "Thank you."

She was thanking him more for Ethan than for the hand, and when he kissed her back, she was sure he understood.

Mary maneuvered her dress into the cab and held her skirts aside while Charles shut the door. "Why sir, what would my husband think about this?"

"He'd think that a slick line like that deserved to get the girl."

"Slick line?"

"A real prime pickup line."

"Pickup line?" Mary started laughing. "Are you going to tell me where we're going on our honeymoon? Are we taking the truck to the airport?"

"No, we're just taking the truck. I found this great place to park. I want to know if making out with a wife is as much fun as —"

In spite of the crowd, Mary leaned in and showed him just how much fun making out with a wife could be.

"Well," she said, moving primly back to her side of the truck, "now that you have the answer to your question, where are we going?"

Ethan turned and smiled at his wife. "We're going on a wild ride, honey."

"I know," Mary Sky Blue Rosenthal Westbrook said with a knowing smile. "I know."

ABOUT THE AUTHOR

Award-winning author **Holly Jacobs** has written over twenty books. She is a lifelong resident of Erie, Pennsylvania and is happily married with four children. She credits her family for everything she knows about love and laughter.

You can visit Holly at:
www.hollysbooks.com
Or mail her at:
P.O. Box 11102
Erie, PA 16524-1102

The employees of Thorndike Press hope you have enjoyed this Large Print book. All our Thorndike, Wheeler, and Kennebec Large Print titles are designed for easy reading, and all our books are made to last. Other Thorndike Press Large Print books are available at your library, through selected bookstores, or directly from us.

For information about titles, please call:
  (800) 223-1244

or visit our Web site at:
  http://gale.cengage.com/thorndike

To share your comments, please write:
  Publisher
  Thorndike Press
  295 Kennedy Memorial Drive
  Waterville, ME 04901